Theatrical Evolution: 1776–1976

by Kenneth Spritz

THE HUDSON RIVER MUSEUM

Why should our thoughts to distant countries roam,
When each refinement may be found at home?

    The Contrast (1787)
    Royall Tyler, "Citizen of the United States"

© 1976 by The Hudson River Museum at
Yonkers, Inc., 511 Warburton Avenue,
Yonkers, New York 10701

Library of Congress Cataloging in
Publication Data

Spritz, Kenneth, 1948–
    Theatrical evolution, 1776–1976

    Bibliography: p.
    1. Theater--United States--History.
I. Title.
PN2221.S6   792'.0973   76-9774
ISBN 0-89062-021-0

The Hudson River Museum acknowledges
with gratitude the support of the National
Endowment for the Arts (a federal agency)
and the New York State Council on the Arts,
whose grants made possible this book and
the exhibition upon which it was based.
Produced by the Publishing Center for
Cultural Resources, 27 West 53 Street, New
York City 10021.

Manufactured in the United States of
America.

Introduction

Throughout the course of our history, the American theatre has been looked upon as a stepchild of the British art form, a second-rate copy dressed in hand-me-downs, waiting to come of age. In the late 18th and early 19th centuries, this outlook was valid from an historical vantage (and, somewhat, from an artistic one). Our theatrical heritage was directly descended from England, and our early attempts were amateurish efforts in comparison to the performances which could be seen at tradition-steeped theatres such as London's Drury Lane. Clearly, there was good reason why British performers and repertoire fully dominated the American stage during this period of ferment and growth.

Nevertheless, the American stage rapidly assumed distinct characteristics. Attitudes, practices, cultural traits, and life styles developed here which were directly related to the harsh experience of the American citizen. And as Americans emerged with an identity that differed from the English, so, too, did their theatre — both in play content and performance style. Early in its history, the American theatre became a proud and adventurous voice for the American people.

There have been numerous attempts to trace all our significant theatre developments back to the London boards. The forms of playwriting, the means of advertising, the acting styles, the architecture, all these elements and more can be put in some perspective with corresponding events in the much more accessible history of the British theatre. But the perspective does not explain the success of such vastly popular American actors as Edwin Forrest, F. S. Chanfrau, and Joseph Jefferson; playwrights like Robert Montgomery Bird, Edward Harrigan, and David Belasco; and plays like *A Glance at New York, Uncle Tom's Cabin,* and *The Contrast.* All reek Americana — a nebulous quality, alive in the blood, but more sensed than understood. Perhaps a case *could* be made for their having British roots — but, oh, how the contemporaneous audiences of those past pinnacles would have roared at the mention of such an idea. The *American* theatre is America's legends and heroes personified — Americans speaking to their countrymen, declaiming their mutual dreams of the future — and hope for us all.

The purpose of this publication and the exhibition upon which it is based is not to jingoistically defend the honor of our national theatre (although that possibility occasionally entered my mind as I leafed

3

through illustrated histories of the world's theatre and found only a chapter or two on our own). It is simply an exploration of extant artifacts in collections throughout our nation which best demonstrate the changing perfomance style, play content, and visual quality of our theatre as it developed from its inception to the present. I set my sights on making as accurate and as visually exciting a compilation as was possible.

I am amazed at the volume of material which has been preserved, both in obvious places for obvious reasons and elsewhere for very personal and sentimental (perhaps, the most valid and dramatic) ones. Yet little use is being made of visual material in the teaching and interpretation of theatre history. Too few of the actors and historians who know that Joseph Jefferson captured the heart of the nation as Rip Van Winkle have seen his portrait; but it is undeniable that a clearer understanding of Jefferson's art can be had from the recorded twinkle in his eye and the stance of his figure than from any explanatory text.

Eclipsed by newer forms our acting styles, production values, technology, architecture — our theatre of the past — has been assimilated into a corps of contemporary work and left largely to graveyard repositories with social historians as caretakers. Thus, men like Edwin Booth, who broke through a stylized tradition of Shakespeare for a deeper, more personal meaning, and Steele MacKaye, a spatial visionary ever dreaming of theatre to come — men like these, their aspirations, and the aspirations of their America — are left unacknowledged.

With our contemporary theatre in a state of constant excitement and change, that is perhaps the way it should be. But, as Royall Tyler puts it in *The Contrast,* "The bold attempt alone demands applause." So the aim here is also to recover what has too often gone unacknowledged.

What follows is intended to spark memories where they can be sparked, to introduce new longing for those moments of the past we can never recover, and to instill an anticipation for the future. It is intended as a tribute to those who have trod the boards in the past and to the artists, technicians, architects, playwrights, musicians, and of course, audiences who loved the theatre that was — and believe in the magic of the theatre of today. It is a salute to the Booths and Barrymores who made it — but equally to the actors now waiting on tables to pay for classes, photos, resumes, and carfare for the one big break that may never come. It is a

4

colorful sampling of a colorful story; but, of course, a totally successful and comprehensive exhibition or book on American theatre could never transcend the limitations of its medium and become one with its subject. Theatre truly exists only through the event.

In the following pages you will find reproductions of objects arranged chronologically. However, this is not intended to serve as a definitive historical reference book. It is for those who wish to gain insight into the American stage through a pleasurable visual experience. There is more that it can provide for those who engage in similar future projects or those who simply want to see more of the same — for visits to several little-known collections named here will reveal hundreds and sometimes thousands of equally noteworthy works.

My criteria for selection were threefold. In each case I asked: what does the work represent? who did the work? and do I like the work? Admittedly, some of the selections fail to do justice to the subject; but I found no better prospects, and omission of the particular performer or play would have amounted to historical injustice. This does not mean that better works do not exist but only that I could not locate nor gain access to them. I hope in all instances that my work here will lead to the uncovering and display of theatrical art and memorabilia of superior quality.

Theatre collections exist for a variety of reasons and contain a staggering diversity of materials. There are the large public research collections containing visual and documentary materials — the Humanities Research Center at the University of Texas, Austin, and the Theatre Collection of the New York Public Library at Lincoln Center, among others. And there are those which are primarily microfilm or reference collections with a few very choice original works — the Theatre Research Institute of Ohio State University, for example. Private collections range from those of dealers (like the Margo Feiden Galleries) representing artists whose subjects are or were of a theatrical nature to the most amazing array of precious theatrical art works and memorabilia I have ever seen — lovingly collected by Franklyn Lenthall and now displayed in Boothbay, Maine at the Boothbay Theatre Museum. And, of course, there are the private caches of the artists themselves — scenic and

II. *The Playbill for this Production*

costume designers, actors, producers, and directors — as well as the unpredictable holdings of art museums and historical societies.

Despite the voluminous visual material on all aspects of the American theatre, research has its difficulties. There is, of course, no catalogue to indicate what exists where, and in some institutions accessioning proceeds so slowly that even the curators don't know the full extent of their holdings. The fact that so much of American's visual theatrical heritage is still in the hands of designers (who are disinclined to donate their works to institutions because of unjust tax laws for artists — especially in light of general museum failure to acknowledge them as the fine artists they are) makes for further difficulty.

Many scenic and costume designs have disappeared. Thought of as working drawings which have served their purpose, they are all too often discarded, leaving only photographs to provide visual evidence of the production. (To designers, scene shop managers, and all concerned, I can only plead — please stop this wasting of our theatrical heritage!) Many works in public or private hands are slowly decomposing due to lack of proper storage or conservation techniques. No blame can be placed in this regard. Even with adequate knowledge, some of our larger collections are burdened with such a body of poorly mounted, stored, and catalogued materials that the time and money to properly preserve their treasures would be beyond even the most persistent efforts.

I have chosen works which illustrate the vast variety of available materials. Some of the works are easily justifiable as "works of art" by museum standards. Some are borderline cases — scenic and costume renderings, in particular, which have too seldom been accepted by art museums and galleries as "legitimate." And some admittedly have no place in the normal context of an art museum, but serve to illustrate a facet of the American theatre more interestingly than artistically superior works. Some materials were essential elements in the development and run of a production — scenic designs, costume designs, drop curtains. Some were used for promotion — posters souvenirs, lobby boards. Some memorialize a performer or performance — figurines or playing cards. Aesthetically, they range from incisive portraits by distinguished artists to the kitsch of a 19th-century commercial figurine.

For those whose imaginations are stimulated by these works, I have included a brief listing of selected publications which would help further knowledge of visual theatrical materials in America. A listing of exhibition lenders is included as a further study guide.

My one hope, as you peruse this book, is that you enjoy it. For if my love and excitement for the works and the theatre they represent is not communicated, then I have failed in the primary responsibility of any performer. In that case, these spirits of our past must wait in the wings for another chance, with another director . . . and another audience.

III. *The Cast and Credits*

As with any theatrical endeavor, the final production can only be as good as the skill and dedication of the individual participants. And so it is with *Theatrical Evolution: 1776–1976*. The "ensemble" for this project numbers in the hundreds. Therefore, I now intend to lead a general, though regretfully inadequate, round of applause for all those who have helped and cannot be singled out in the following credits. To those who cared, this project is truly as much yours as mine.

The exhibition on which this publication is based was my brainchild. At its inception I had no idea of whether it could be satisfactorily completed, and even less of how to go about it. Donald M. Halley, Jr., the director of the Hudson River Museum, who gave me the go-ahead and stood by me, encouraged me, and supported me throughout its development, has proven himself to be no mere "fair weather friend," and for that I am extremely grateful.

Seeing the potential for such an endeavor is a far cry from being able to actually proceed. For the vision and generosity that permitted me to bring the project to completion, I wish to thank the National Endowment for the Arts and the New York State Council on the Arts.

Instrumental in guiding me through the muddy fields of historical interpretation with common-sense advice and suggestions were Prof. Brooks MacNamara of New York University, Monroe Fabian of the National Portrait Gallery, Franklyn Lenthall of the Boothbay Theatre Museum, and Miles Kreuger of the Institute of the American Musical. A special acknowledgment must also go to Prof. Travis Bogard of the University of California at Berkeley for first introducing me to the wonders of the American stage via the genius of Eugene O'Neill.

7

And for doing a protean share of work on this book, as well as giving me continually helpful advice and suggestions for the exhibition, I wish to thank Mike Gladstone and his staff at the Publishing Center for Cultural Resources.

To all the members of the Hudson River Museum staff who assisted me in this project well beyond the normal course of their duties, I wish to extend my respect and appreciation. Particular mention must go to Thom Loughman for photography, Edith Sakell and Doris Crawford for publicity and public relations, K. K. Zutter and Janet Ohlsen for programming and special events (through the education department), Donald Werner for design, Sutherland McColley and Judy Matson for registration of the works, and, especially, Pauline Leontovich and Joan Walker, two typists extraordinaire, for abilities to decipher illegible scrawl that are matched only by their willingness to assist when the crunch is on.

My thanks go especially to my primary assistants on the research and development of this project. First and foremost is Arline Weishar, whom I have found it an extreme pleasure to work with and whose contributions cannot be overestimated. My wife, Kate Schaefer, provided valuable research and support in a very trying period. Ruben Marcello, Debra Steinfeld, and Peter Goldsmith all made valuable contributions in locating and researching important works. Joshua Karton not only wrote the scripts for related multimedia and video presentations but also oversaw their production. Video Life Associates provided technical expertise for video production. To all of them, I express unreserved gratitude.

Finally, there are the numerous lenders who not only gave works for the exhibition but advice, support, and suggestions for locating additional works. They are named elsewhere, but a note of thanks is also due to the many publications who ran my appeals for information.

My closing kudos must go the theatre-going public, both past and present. Without it, there would be no American theatre. And no audience for *Theatrical Evolution: 1776–1976.*

Kenneth Spritz

Prologue

*. . . and we observe that all men
find pleasure in imitations.*

Aristotle's Poetics

*Interior of the Pantheon Theatre, London;
engraving by Wise after drawing by G.
Jones, 1815; Cooper-Hewitt Museum of
Design, Smithsonian Institution*

From earliest time man has imitated life, expanded upon life, and
improved his life through the evolution of his theatrical activities. From
the earliest tribal celebrations to Sophocles, to Seneca, to Shakespeare, to
Sheridan, and on down through the ages and cultures of man, our
theatrical practices have been vital building blocks that served as a
necessary popular voice for the ethics, morality, culture, and dignity of
mankind.

Though playhouses existed in a particular form for a particular brief
period, the reason for their existence remains unchanged. Theatre has
always been and will remain an integral part of our lives. This is an
examination of one brief part of theatre history — that of the American
theatre. Look at it and wonder. Let it transport you back in time. And
think of it as the beginning of a long, illustrious, and ennobling tradition.

Wilson sculp

The Craft from the Continent

The theatre that was brought to the colonies from England was, on the one hand, primitive and rudimentary and, on the other, rich in centuries of tradition. Naturally, the best performers on Britain's boards spurned the hinterlands of colonial America for the richer and more civilized audiences of their country. Performing in such theatres as the Drury Lane or the Pantheon would have been a much more seductive lure than any of the earliest specially constructed theatres in America, let alone the prospect of a crudely converted commercial space.

But the colonists, who lived a hard life, clamored for the few pleasures available — theatre being one of them. Despite periodic governmental and religious prohibitions against performance, our earliest companies (crude though they may have been) found an appreciative — and growing — audience. These troupes moved from town to town as audience demand necessitated, and performed in whatever space could accommodate them. Eventually, new theatres were built. Crude at first, these buildings followed the traditions of theatre architecture in England, and gave us our first testing ground for later generations of American-born actors and playwrights.

Tightrope walker on stage; engraving by
Alexander Wilson, c.1800; Cooper-Hewitt
Museum of Design, Smithsonian Institution

WILD OATS.

John Henry as Ephraim Smooth in Wild Oats; *engraving by C. Tiebout, c.1780; The Harvard Theatre Collection*

In the late 17th and early 18th centuries, Puritan opposition to theatre and other "painted vanities" made life very difficult for our early performers. The colonial records of Massachusetts, Rhode Island, Pennsylvania, South Carolina, and New York all show official protests against performance. Despite this opposition, theatre prevailed through perseverance and chicanery, often masking performances as "moral lectures" and, sometimes, as in the case of *Wild Oats,* even satirizing the moralizations of its persecutors. Ultimately, the need for theatre allowed it to outlive not only religious persecution but Congressional injunction, riot, disease, and numerous fires.

12

Plumstead's (or Plumsted's) warehouse,
Philadelphia — the first building used as a
theatre in America; engraving, 1754;
Hoblitzelle Theatre Arts Collections,
courtesy of the Humanities Research Center,
The University of Texas at Austin

Our very earliest actors worked in whatever space was available in the town they played — brewery, warehouse, and inn being likely possibilities. Generally, they stayed from a single performance to a week or more before traveling on in search of a new audience. Eventually, theatres were built to specifically accommodate the players, usually in larger cities with a relatively liberal outlook on the performing arts. Among the early theatre centers were Richmond, Philadelphia, Newport, Rhode Island, and New York. During the first quarter of the 19th century, the Park Theatre of New York City and the New (Chestnut Street) Theatre of Philadelphia vied for national eminence, but between fierce competition for audiences and the ever-present hazard of theatre fires (which continued to the 20th century), there was rapid development of new and better theatres in these and other major cities.

13

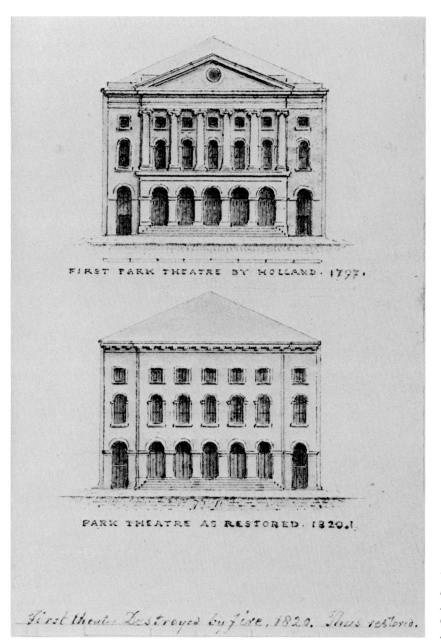

FIRST PARK THEATRE BY HOLLAND. 1797.

PARK THEATRE AS RESTORED. 1820.

First theatre Destroyed by fire, 1820. Thus restored.

The Park Theatre, New York;
before-and-after exterior elevations by
Alexander Jackson Davis, 1820;
Cooper-Hewitt Museum of Design,
Smithsonian Institution

Inside View of the New Theatre. Philadelphia.

The New Theatre, Philadelphia; print by W. Ralph, 1794; Cooper-Hewitt Museum of Design, Smithsonian Institution

The burning of the Richmond Theatre; color lithograph, 1812; Hoblitzelle Theatre Arts Collections, courtesy of the Humanities Research Center, The University of Texas at Austin

NEW THEATRE.

Wednesday Evening, January 5th, 1803,

Will be Presented, a celebrated COMEDY, in 5 acts, called THE

MERCHANT OF VENICE.

(Written by SHAKESPEARE.)

Duke,	- - -	Mr. MORRIS.
Antnonio,	- - -	Mr. WARREN.
Bassanio,	(1st time)	Mr. WOOD.
Gratiano,	- - -	Mr. BERNARD.
Lorenzo,	(with songs	Mr. FOX.
Solarino,	- - -	Mr. CAIN.
Salanio,	- - -	Mr. USHER.
Shylock,	*(first time on this stage)*	Mr. GREEN.
Tubal,	- - -	Mr. MILBOURNE.
Launcelot,	- - -	Mr. BLISSETT.
Old Gobbo,	- - -	Mr. FRANCIS
Balthazar,	- - -	Mr. WHEATLY.
Leonardo,	- - -	Mr. DURANG.
Portia,	- - -	Mrs. BARRETT.
Jessica,	- - -	Mrs. JONES.
Nerissa,	- - -	Mrs. FRANCIS.

To which will be added, a COMIC OPERA, in two acts, called

THE RIVAL SOLDIERS;
OR, SPRIGS OF LAUREL.

(Written by O'Keefe, author of the Poor Soldier, Highland Reel, &c.)

Captain Cruizer,	- - -	Mr. Usher.
Lenox,	- - -	Mr. Cain.
Major Tactic,	- - -	Mr. Jones.
Sinclair,	- - -	Mr. Fox.
Nipperkin,	- - -	Mr. Bernard.
Corporal,	- - -	Mr. Durang.
The Little Midshipman,	- - -	Miss Solomon.
Mary Tactic,	- - -	Mrs. Jones.

BOX, one Dollar. PIT, three quarters of a Dollar. And GALLERY, half a Dollar.

☞ Doors to be opened at a quarter past 5 and the CURTAIN to rise at a quarter past 6 o'clock.

⁎ Tickets to be had at H. and P. RICE's book-store, No. 16, South Second Street, and at the OFFICE adjoining the THEATRE.

⁎ Places in the Boxes to be taken of Mr. EVANS, in the front of the theatre from 10 till 2, and on the days of PERFORMANCE from 10 till 4 o'clock.

The Merchant of Venice *at the New Theatre; playbill dated January 5, 1803; collection of Philip H. Likes II (photo: Thom Loughman)*

The Hallam Company, managed by Lewis Hallam, Sr., arrived in America from England in 1752 — bankrupt. As our first "professional" company they form the foundation upon which our national theatre was established, changing their name to the Old American Company following Hallam's death. They were responsible for the construction of some of our earliest theatre buildings (the Southwark and Chestnut Street Theatres of Philadelphia among them) as well as the production of our first successful American play, *The Contrast.* The playbill for the colonial audience generally consisted of a comedic prelude, a major work (often Shakespeare), and a musical afterpiece in the vein of Durang's hornpipe. The performances were crude and often makeshift, but the audiences took great delight and pride in "their" company and the entertainment they provided.

"John Durang in Character of a Hornpipe";
watercolor by John Durang, c.1800;
Historical Society of York County

Nancy Hallam as Imogen disguised as the
boy, Fidele, in Cymbeline; *O/C by Charles*
Willson Peale, 1771; Colonial
Williamsburg

Expansion and Development

The period that followed the War of 1812 was a time of developing political identity for Americans. Our country was forming a world image of itself as a proud, free, strong, and ever-growing nation. Free enterprise allowed the more enterprising to form an upper crust on the early melting pot of American society and the resulting class-oriented social structure gave fuel to the resentment Jacksonian Democrats harbored for anything aristocratic and, by implication, remotely British.

During these troubled and exciting times, an actor named Edwin Forrest rose to become the first native-born American tragedian to achieve recognition both here and abroad. His career followed the growth of the nation as it expanded to include the Louisiana Purchase. He performed in dim and musty firetraps seemingly thrown up overnight to accommodate his performances, and he performed in palatial new playhouses built in every major city in the country. He saw theatres burn — and he saw bigger and better ones rise. And he saw other Americans take to the stage in greater numbers and with more finely honed skills than ever before. Though the British still dominated the American stage, America was forming a voice of its own. Wherever Americans settled, theatre followed — either because of public demand or the actor-manager's scent of money to be made. Young actors traveled the hinterland circuits to sharpen their skills on the stages of early playhouses like the New Orleans American Theatre before facing the more critical audiences of Philadelphia, Boston, or New York. Without this "frontier circuit," the Edwin Forrests and Edwin Booths would have had a much more difficult time gaining acceptance and collecting the accolades they deserved.

Paint shop of a New York theatre. The appearance of the early 19th-century theatrical paint shop was essentially the same as the one shown in this watercolor by Charles Witham, c.1880; Theatre and Music Collection of the Museum of the City of New York (photo: Thom Loughman)

*The American Theatre, New Orleans; O/C
by Auguste Norieri, 1890 (from lithograph
by Reinagle, 1833–34); Louisiana State
Museum*

The Park Theatre in New York City eventually achieved artistic dominance as the leading theatre in America. It was not until the opening of the Bowery Theatre on October 23, 1826, that a rival came into existence. The Bowery, seating 3,500 people, was generally acknowledged to be the grandest theatre the country had yet seen — with tasteful decorations and enclosed gas lighting new to New York theatre-goers. The Bowery also proved to have a resiliency unlike any other American theatre. In the course of nearly a century it survived four devastating fires, introducing many of our greatest classical performers and providing a continuing center for vaudeville, burlesque, pantomime, farce, and melodrama, before being burned for the last time in 1929. We will never see her like again.

The Bowery Theater, New York; color engraving published by Rawden, Wright and Company, 1828; Cooper-Hewitt Museum of Design, Smithsonian Institution

The burning of the American Theatre, New York; color engraving by H. B. Robinson, 1836; New-York Historical Society

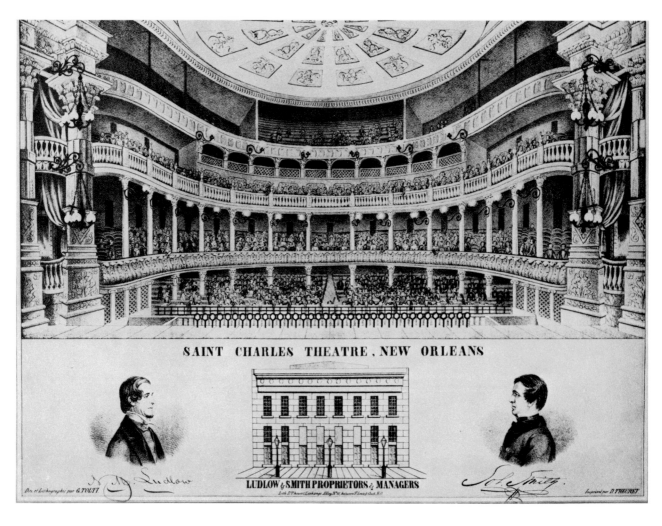

SAINT CHARLES THEATRE, NEW ORLEANS

LUDLOW & SMITH PROPRIETORS & MANAGERS

The (second) St. Charles Theatre, New Orleans, c.1842; lithograph; Library of Congress

The Western theatre circuit developed in much the same way as theatre in the East. Mobile, New Orleans, and St. Louis (among others) all had major theatres early in the 19th century. The (second) St. Charles Theatre in New Orleans was built on the ruins of the St. Charles Theatre which burned in 1842. When completed, like the Bowery before it and numerous theatres to follow, it was described as "The Most Elegant Looking Auditory in the Country."

22

Until the mid-19th century, British actors still dominated the American stage. America was, as yet, too short of manpower to afford many able bodies for such an "idle" occupation, but Americans who did take to the boards were fortunate that actors of real quality began to cross the ocean in search of the growing (and more affluent) audience developing in America.

George Frederick Cooke was the first truly great English actor to arrive in this country — according to legend, shanghaied by an American manager while in a helpless drunken stupor. His mode of arrival notwithstanding, the country saw the likes of a performance previously unmatched when he performed Richard III at the Park Theatre. He was idolized by his fellow countryman and thespian, Edmond Kean — who, in turn, was studied and admired during his American performances by our own Edwin Forrest.

George Frederick Cooke as Richard III; hand tinted engraving by Dighton, 1800; The Boothbay Theatre Museum, Franklyn Lenthall, Curator (photo: Thom Loughman)

Edmond Kean as King John; engraving by P. Roberts, c.1810; The Boothbay Theatre Museum, Franklyn Lenthall, Curator (photo: Thom Loughman)

Charles Kemble as Cromwell; engraving by J. Sartain, c.1830; Prints Division, The New York Public Library, Astor, Lenox and Tilden Foundations

Fanny Kemble as painted by Henry Inman; mezzotint by S. Arlent Edwards, c.1840; The Boothbay Theatre Museum, Franklyn Lenthall, Curator (photo: Thom Loughman)

24

Junius Brutus Booth in Brutus; *O/C by John Neagle, 1827; Theatre and Music Collection of the Museum of the City of New York (photo: Thom Loughman)*

Still later, came Charles and Fanny Kemble, father and daughter, admired both by the public and their fellow actors for their "benefit" performances to raise money for sick, indigent, or retired performers.

On October 5, 1821, Junius Brutus Booth first appeared on an American stage (Park Theatre) and launched the Booth-Drew-Barrymore dynasty that would gain international respect for the American theatre for more than a century.

Charlotte and Susan Cushman as Romeo and Juliet; Staffordshire figurine, c.1850–60; The Boothbay Theatre Museum, Franklyn Lenthall, Curator (photo: Thom Lougham)

James H. Hackett as Falstaff; Staffordshire figurine, c.1840–50; The Boothbay Theatre Museum, Franklyn Lenthall, Curator (photo: Thom Loughman)

During the 1830s and 1840s, American actors began to come into their own. James Henry Hackett, born in 1800 in New York City, was our first great comic actor, best known for his interpretation of Falstaff and the introduction of Rip Van Winkle to our stage. Charlotte Cushman made her debut in Boston in 1835. In the course of a forty-year career, she was recognized as the greatest actress America had yet produced (and she may well still rank as the greatest American actress of all time). The darling of critics on both sides of the ocean, she toured this country and England, receiving high acclaim for such roles as Lady Macbeth and Romeo.

Ira Aldridge, born an American, lived in a time when Blacks were not commonly accepted as performers by the American theatre-going public. In 1826, billed as the "African Roscius," he made his British debut at the Royalty Theatre as Othello. From that time until his death in 1867, he had a distinguished career as one of the greatest actors of his day — on the European stage. He never returned here.

Ira Aldridge as Othello; engraving, c.1827; The Boothbay Theatre Museum, Franklyn Lenthall, Curator (photo: Thom Loughman)

English Ira Aldridge playbill of 1827; The Boothbay Theatre Museum, Franklyn Lenthall, Curator (photo: Thom Loughman)

Theatre-Royal, Manchester.

For the BENEFIT of the
African Roscius,

And his last Appearance this Season.

Miss F. H. KELLY'S Second Week.

This present Saturday, Feb. 24th, 1827,

Will be performed Sheridan's Tragedy of

PIZARRO.

PERUVIANS.

The Part of ROLLA — — by THE AFRICAN ROSCIUS

Ataliba	Mr. POWELL	Huscah		Mr. MORELLI
Orozumbo	Mr. HAMMOND	Orano		Mr. SEFTON
The High Priest	Mr. BENSON			
Huaipo	Mr. SMITH	Fernando		Miss JONES
Tupac	Miss E. RADCLIFFE	Cora		Miss R. PUNLEY

Priestesses of the Sun — Messrs. Taylor, Clarke, Radcliffe, Lockwood, Rose, Miss Field, Miss Holdaway, Miss Barrett, Miss Radcliffe, and Miss Wallis.

SPANIARDS.

Pizarro	Mr. RAYMOND	Gonzalo		Mr. LOCKWOOD
Alonzo	Mr. HUNT	Gomez		Mr. BENWELL
Las Casas	Mr. ANDREWS	Davilla		Mr. WILTON
Valverde	Mr. LEAVES	Sentinel		Mr. PORTEUS
Almagro	Mr. HAMBLETON			

The Part of ELVIRA — — by Miss F. H. KELLY.

In the course of the Evening,

THE AFRICAN ROSCIUS,

Will Sing the Comic Songs of

" What a terrible Life am I led "

" LET ME WHEN MY HEART'S A-SINKING " & " A GREAT WAY OFF AT SEA "

To conclude with the favourite Musical Entertainment called

THE PADLOCK.

The Part of MUNGO — (the Black Servant) — by THE AFRICAN ROSCIUS.

Don Diego	Mr. ANDREWS	Leonora		Miss FIELD
Leander	Mr. BENSON	Ursula		Mrs. TAYLOR
Scholars	Messrs. Wilton & Sefton			

On MONDAY next, will be produced for the first time here, the New Drama of LUKE THE LABOURER. After which CATHERINE & PETRUCHIO. The part of CATHERINE, by Miss F. H. KELLY. To conclude with

THE PILOT.

Tickets and Places to be taken of Mr. ELAND, at the Box-office of the Theatre, from Eleven till Two o'clock.
Prices of Admission, Boxes, 4s.—Upper Boxes, 3s.—Pit, 2s.—Gallery, 1s.
Doors will be opened at Half-past Six, and the performance will commence precisely at Seven.

Printed by J. PHENIX, 14, Bow Street.

Edwin Forrest; O/C by John Neagle, c.1840–50; The Brander Matthews Collection, Columbia University (photo: Thom Loughman)

William Charles Macready; O/C by Chester Harding, c.1830–40; Sleepy Hollow Restorations (photo: Thom Loughman)

William Charles Macready; hand colored and appliqued engraving, c.1849; Theatre and Music Collection of the Museum of the City of New York (photo: Thom Loughman)

One of his contemporary critics looked upon the acting of Edwin Forrest as that of a "vast animal bewildered by a little grain of genius." Another, James Henry Hackett, wrote that he "infused into his last act of *Othello* a degree of manly tenderness, refined sensibility, and touching melancholy, so true to Nature and Art, that his performance . . . afforded me exquisite and unalloyed gratification." Though Forrest may not have shared the universal respect of Charlotte Cushman or the later Edwin Booth, he was a man who stirred emotions both on and off stage and who captured the imagination of the world.

His early years as an actor were marked by poverty, hardship, and an ambition too great for his untrained talent. Though often criticized for the "ravings" of his extremely physical performances, he won acclaim in such demanding roles as Othello, Macbeth, and King Lear. Seeking new materials for his distinct acting style, he initiated the first American playwriting competition — which gave rise to John Augustus Stone's *Metamora* (or the *Last of the Wampanoags),* the first successful play with an American Indian focal character.

Forrest twice went to London — in 1836 with some success, and again in 1845, when he was received with hostility he attributed to the machinations of his British stage rival, William Charles Macready.

Macready was the eminent tragedian of his day — rivaled in acclaim only by Edmond Kean. After Kean's death, his position was unparalleled anywhere in the world. The young Edwin Forrest was an ardent admirer, and they developed a cordial association.

The feud which developed between Macready and Forrest stemmed from the press. Nationalistic critics compared their styles and interpretations until each was sure of a conspiracy to prevent his performing in the other's country. Stories abound of Forrest hissing at a Macready performance and of Macready's manipulation of newspaper editors. The relationship was anything but cordial in 1849, when Macready unfortunately chose once again to perform in America.

Mr. Macready, as Sir Reginald, Front de Bœuf.

Americans with sufficient means to attend the theatre regularly supported Forrest — bad-mannered and coarse though he may have been — as a symbol of national pride. The openly slanderous campaigns that Forrest and Macready launched against each other on the stage and in the press in 1849 might have promoted ticket sales at another time. But in 1849 the political mood in New York was such that their rivalry became the catalyst for broad conflict — Forrest's "working-class" Democrats vs. the Macready "aristocracy."

The evening of May 10, 1849 Macready was performing at the Astor Place Opera House and Forrest at the Broadway Theatre. When Forrest, as Macbeth, acclaimed, "What rhubarb, senna or what purgative drug will scour these English hence?" his audience rose and cheered. When Macready attempted to perform as Macbeth he was interrupted by the crashing of glass and bricks and the rattle of musketry. The Astor Place Riot had begun. Questions remain as to why and how. The only certainty is in the statistics: two hundred and ten soldiers confronted a crowd of ten to twenty thousand — and seventeen were killed. Macready barely escaped — by being disguised as a rioter and smuggled out — to return to England. Forrest never regained the support of the moneyed American audience — although he did become the champion of the masses. He lived a bitter and lonely existence until his death in 1872, but he stayed on the stage until his end.

With the death of Edwin Forrest came the end of a rocky and tempestuous theatrical childhood. America — and her theatre — had come of age.

GREAT RIOT AT THE ASTOR PLACE OPERA HOUSE, NEW YORK.

ON THURSDAY EVENING MAY 10TH 1849.

Great Riot at the Astor Place Opera
House; *engraving by Currier and Ives,
1849; Lent by the Library of Congress*

[handwritten signatures of actors]

The Civil War was an interruption, but hardly a deterrent, to the American theatre. If anything, it gave our playwrights more subjects about which to write — more ideas with which the growing urban audience's varied minds could grapple. Though foreign plays were still imported, American themes — slavery, urban problems, native folk heroes — were in strong demand. The number of theatres boomed in every city to accommodate the wide array of entertainments demanded by a diverse and escape-hungry public.

The "popular entertainments" — vaudeville, burlesque, minstrelry, and circus — which had previously been more rurally oriented found acceptance with such establishments as those managed by P. T. Barnum and Tony Pastor. As the demand for spectacle grew with the refined presentation of melodrama, competitive innovations in scenic and lighting effects were commonplace. The "smash hits" were the most spectacular shows — like *Uncle Tom's Cabin* and *The Black Crook*. Although the country now reached from coast to coast, New York was becoming the theatre capital, where stars were born and fortunes could be made and lost on the stage.

The classics, particularly Shakespeare, were not forgotten. They had a staunch friend in Edwin Booth, perhaps the greatest of American tragedians, who personified all that it was to be a great actor and a great man. Though different from Edwin Forrest, both in his style of acting and his style of living, he stands as the next major stepping stone in the development of our contemporary American theatre.

Memorial poster; lithograph, c.1870; George J. Goodstadt, Inc. (photo: Thom Loughman)

33

J. W. Wallack, Lester Wallack, and John Brougham in The Merchant of Venice *performed at Wallack's Theatre, December 9, 1858; watercolor by Victor Moblard; Theatre and Music Collection of the Museum of the City of New York (photo: Thom Loughman)*

In any survey of the "golden age of the actor" the natural starting point must be the Wallack family of actor-managers whose longevity and continued artistic success in the theatre made "Wallack's" a trademark of excellence. Beginning with James W. Wallack in 1818, there was a Wallack on the New York stage for the better part of a century to set an example for America with good acting and solid production values. From 1861 to 1882, Wallack's Theatre boasted the finest stock company in the nation. The theatre finally closed in 1915 — to be demolished and replaced by an office building. An epilogue spoken at the end of the last performance there is fitting tribute to the historic house: "The play is done, and with it another page / Of history is turned . . . / And as the weeks go by, will rise and rise / A titan monster stretching to the skies, / Yet tho' by measured cubits is outspan / The Woolworth tower or Metropolitan. . . . / 'Twill never reach the heights Elysian, / Won by this house that Lester Wallack built."

34

To have great actors one must have great plays, and a good deal of the responsibility for the 19th-century repertoire lies with Dion Boucicault. He arrived in America from Dublin in 1853, and proceeded to create many of the most famous and popular plays of his day, including *The Octoroon* — a play about slavery, *Suil A Mor* — a play of Ireland, and our most popular adaptation of Rip Van Winkle. Though not terribly inventive regarding the details of plot (most of his stories being borrowed or adapted), he was most efficient at devising exciting stage business and melodramatic effects. An actor and businessman as well as a playwright, Boucicault was responsible for devising the first "combination system" with several companies of actors on the road with the same play at the same time — a most profitable arrangement!

Dion Boucicault's Suil A More (*or* Life in Galway); *lithograph poster, c.1870; George J. Goodstadt, Inc. (photo: Thom Loughman)*

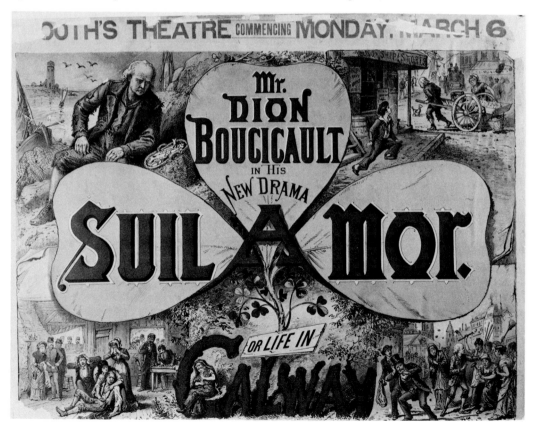

Joseph Jefferson as Rip Van Winkle; O/C by George Waters, c.1885–90; Sleepy Hollow Restorations

Joseph Jefferson as Bob Acres in The Rivals; *O/C by Frank Eugene Smith, c.1880; The Brander Matthews Collection, Columbia University (photo: Thom Loughman)*

Boucicault also gave Joseph Jefferson his greatest boost to fame. Jefferson (1829–1905) had already had some success and notoriety as an actor in *The Octoroon* and *Our American Cousin,* when Boucicault gave him a new adaptation of *Rip Van Winkle* in 1864. He continued to play the Rip Van Winkle role to great critical and popular success for over 15 years. Later, his touring production of Sheridan's *The Rivals* with a cast that included Mrs. John Drew was equally successful.

37

*Lettersheet view of the Jenny Lind Theatre,
San Francisco, c.1851; California
Historical Society*

Scenic rendering for the dairy scene in Our
American Cousin *by Tom Taylor, c.1858;
Theatre Collection, The New York Public
Library, Astor, Lenox and Tilden
Foundations (photo: Thom Loughman)*

Playbill for Laura Keene in Our
American Cousin, *April 14, 1865; The
National Parks Service — Ford's Theatre
National Historic Site (photo: Thom
Loughman)*

The third Jenny Lind Theatre was built after the destruction by fire
of two earlier Jenny Lind houses. It gave San Francisco its first fully
equipped luxury playhouse, and established the city as a Western center
worthy of our finest actors — although Jenny Lind herself never
performed there. By 1861, San Francisco could boast two American
theatres, one French theatre, and a circus.

Our American Cousin is associated with one of the most infamous acts in American history — the assassination of President Lincoln. The play starred Laura Keene, an actress of considerable talent who was known in addition as a manager of artistic sensibility and shrewd business sense. Playing with her was E. A. Sothern, brought to fame in the role of Lord Dundreary, and Joseph Jefferson, a rising star who would later reach full glory as Rip Van Winkle. The play opened at Miss Keene's New Theatre in New York, then traveled to Ford's Theatre in Washington in 1865.

Portrait of Edwin Booth; O/C by Eastman Johnson, c.1875; anonymous lender

Edwin Booth, son of Junius Brutus Booth and brother of John Wilkes and Junius Brutus, Jr., was our most illustrious tragedian. His reputation was made in Boston and New York, but he achieved acclaim as far afield as England and California (although a poor business sense destined his threatres to financial failure). In the roles of Shylock, Hamlet, Iago, and Lear he was unsurpassed.

His ability to enter social circles normally closed to theatre people induced him to form the Players, a club in which men of the business world mingled with those of the arts. Said Booth at the formal opening, "Although our vocations are various, I greet you all as brother Players. At this supreme moment of my life, it is my happy privilege to assume the character of host, to welcome you to the house wherein I hope that we for

40

Edwin Booth as Iago; O/C by Thomas Hicks,
1864; collection of Pearl and Carl Cohen
(photo: Thom Loughman)

Interior of Booth's Theatre showing the
setting for Romeo and Juliet; *watercolor*
by Charles Witham, c.1870–80; Theatre
and Music Collection of the Museum of the
City of New York (photo: Thom Loughman)

many years and our legitimate successors for at least a thousand generations, may assemble, for friendly intercourse and intellectual recreation."

Edwin Booth died in 1893. His epitaph — from the Book of Jeremiah — is a fitting tribute and a just memorial: "I will turn their mourning into joy and will comfort them and make them rejoice."

On April 14, 1865 John Wilkes Booth, the mad brother of Edwin in the cast of *Our American Cousin*, performed the dastardly act that shook the nation and plunged it into mourning. Edwin Booth announced his retirement from the stage soon thereafter, but the public had enough common sense and compassion to recognize his innocence —and, by popular appeal, he returned to the stage to continue his long and illustrious career. Ford's Theatre, however, remained closed until 1967, when it was reopened as a National Historic Site.

Architectural elevations for the restoration of Ford's Theatre, Washington, D.C.; The National Parks Service — Ford's Theatre National Historic Site (photo: Thom Loughman)

Interior of Augustin Daly's Theatre;
engraving, 1879; Cooper-Hewitt Museum
of Design, Smithsonian Institution

Satin playbill for Daly's London Theatre;
Theatre Collection, The Free Library of
Philadelphia (photo: Thom Loughman)

Just as Wallack's Threatre is the natural beginning for an examination of the age of the actor, Augustin Daly is fitting focus for the transition to the era of the manager — when the businessman dominated the theatre. Daly did not conform to any mold. Although not an actor, he possessed theatrical sensibilities far beyond that of most thespians; and as a manager he did not go to the fiscal extremes of later producers seeking secure profits. Daly started as a critic in a time when newspapers were burgeoning to satisfy the rapidly expanding immigrant and working-class population. Although he admired the quality of the Wallack productions he saw, he knew that the prevailing focus on "stars" was often detrimental to the sense of the play. The opening of his own theatre launched a career that eliminated the star system, introduced a more realistic and visually exciting staging, and developed an "ensemble" which trained actors, managers, and playwrights who subsequently went on to great individual success.

Theatre was primarily an urban venture in the 19th century — needing specifically designed spaces and large amounts of capital to be properly produced. At the same time, "popular amusements" increased to satisfy a rural need for escape through entertainment. On showboats such as this, one could see everything from circus acts to minstrel shows, from light operettas to comic clog dancing. It was truly entertainment for the people, easy to produce (at least in its early stages) and readily transportable. As national transportation improved, however, the number of showboats decreased and their entertainments and theatrical diversions settled within the cities or traveled on the newly developed roadways and rails.

T. D. "Jim Crow" Rice, was our first black-faced minstrel. Covering his features with burnt cork, Rice would do a shuffling dance and sing: "Wheel about and turn about/An' do jist so/An' ebery time I wheel about/I jump Jim Crow."

This man and his song were to be the foundation of the most popular form of American entertainment from 1840 to 1880 — the minstrel show. Though probably offensive to today's audiences, the shows were vastly successful both here and later in England, where this ceramic pitcher was produced. Minstrels performed in halls or tents rather than in theatres. Initially "burnt cork" black-faces, they eventually gave rise to some real Black minstrel companies among the hundreds that traversed America in the minstrel's heyday.

The Floating Palace showboat; color lithograph, 1852; Theatre Collection, The Free Library of Philadelphia (photo: Thom Loughman)

44

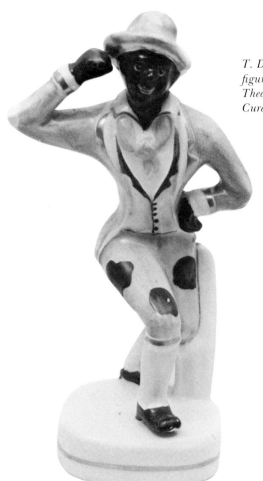

T. D. "Jim Crow" Rice; Staffordshire
figurine, c.1840–50; The Boothbay
Theatre Museum, Franklyn Lenthall,
Curator (photo: Thom Loughman)

Staffordshire minstrel jug from a set of three
produced in 1870 by Beech, Unwin and
Co.; The Boothbay Theatre Museum,
Franklyn Lenthall, Curator (photo: Thom
Loughman)

The Panoramas of
Lima and Thebes
ARE NOW EXHIBITING, DAY AND EVENING,

At the Rotunda, Corner of Prince and Mercer Streets, Broadway, opposite Niblo's Garden.

THE PANORAMA OF LIMA.

This magnificent picture covers a circle of 10,000 square feet, and embraces a bird's-eye view of the City of Lima, taken from the top of an observatory in the centre. The great Cathedral—the numerous Churches, Convents and Monasteries—the broad and beautiful Plaza which surrounds the City—the Port of Callao, with the Pacific Ocean stretching as far as the eye can reach—and lastly, the great Cordilleras raising their lofty peaks, and rising one above the other, until they mingle in the distance with the blue horizon, are the prominent objects embraced in the view. Persons who have visited this picture, pronounce it the most splendid, both as a work of art, and for the rich and varied scenery it embraces, that has ever been exhibited in this country.

Lima, the capital of Peru, was founded in 1535 by Pizarro, as the future capital of the Spanish conquests in the land of the Incas. It arose, and has since continued to be one of the richest and most populous cities of America. Its population in 1810 was 87,000. In beauty of situation, fertility of soil, and mildness of climate, it is unrivalled; though its continual earthquakes more than counterbalance these, and render a residence there of great danger. The city is surrounded by a wall of calcined bricks, 9 feet in thickness and 18 feet high, with seven principal gateways. There are 355 streets, all of which are perfectly straight, though generally narrow. It contains 25 convents, 14 monasteries and 6 institutions where the mass do not profess absolute seclusion. The charitable institutions embrace 7 large hospitals and two convalescencies; in fact, it has been said, that no city in the world distributed so many alms as this.

OPINIONS OF THE PRESS.

Panorama of Lima—Mr. Catherwood has laid the community under due obligations by furnishing another subject of innocent and profitable amusement. It is not invested with the same ancient and sacred associations as the Panorama of Jerusalem, it is more elegantly executed, and has a far more extensive and variegated field for the eye. In fact few places in the world furnish such a subject as Lima for a panoramic representation.

We learn from Mr. Brigham, (Secretary of the Bible Society,) who spent some time in Lima, that the picture is executed with remarkable fidelity, presenting objects as they actually exist. Our citizens, therefore, can see the old splendid "city of the kings," with its grand and beautiful scenery, without a journey round Cape Horn, or a safety voyage through the Isthmus of Mexico. All can be substantially seen in Prince-street, New-York. We doubt not that this exactly will excel the most beautiful of the spectatory presented.—N. Y. Observer.

Panorama of Lima.—The Panorama of Lima is unquestionably one of the most splendid paintings ever exhibited in this country. It represents the beautiful and smoking ruins and of the observatories, where you see the cloud Cathedral, the towers of San Francisco and San Domingo, together with numerous painted spires and temples of the various convents and churches, amidst the growth of orange and lime trees in the surrounding country. The grandeur of the scenery and more enjoyed And a which are seen in the distance, very much heighten the effect of the scene. The magnitude of our great city of Lima, the antique costume of the people which puts one in the estate, with every appearance of life and society, all conspire to make this picture one of surpassing interest; which all lovers of scenery and art will not fail to visit and examine for themselves.—Zion's Watchman.

Panorama of Lima.—The most grand panoramic picture of Lima lately put up in place of the panorama of Jerusalem, is a much more imposing and attractive representation than the latter, in every thing even its excellence. The city of Lima, with its Cathedral, its convent and splendid churches and convents, and above all in the grandeur of the scenery that surrounds it, is one of the most striking objects presented upon this continent, and this painting is in many points superior to any thing of the kind that it has been our lot to look at. The mountains of everlasting snows seen in the distance, and their intervening space, some of which appear to approach almost to the walls of the city, form a prominent feature in the picture, and the houses, grounds, gardens, public squares, the city cemetery, seen in the distant valley of the Rimac—the road to Callao, that plant itself, the rocky islands of the coast, and finally the broad blue waters of the Pacific, are not only beautiful, but sublime. It so chanced while we were looking at this painting a few evenings since, that two gentlemen were present who had resided several years in Lima, and without knowing that they were overheard, they were expressing their delight and astonishment at the wonderful accuracy with which the most minute points in the picture were delineated. It is well worthy of a visit from every one who lives, who may chance to spend a day in New York.—N. Y. Gazette.

The Panorama of Lima is a most splendid specimen of the power of art to bring before the eye of the observer a city and surrounding country, in a manner to cause him to think, for the moment, that it is a reality he is looking on from some observatory in the midst of the city, and viewing the streets, temples, convents, palaces, areas, sites, the towering San Christoval, and the distant snow-capped Cordilleras. It is one of those attractions which afford instruction as well as pleasure, and ought, on that account, to be patronized and encouraged.—Advocate and Journal.

Panorama of Lima—If our readers wish to view a vivid representation of some of the grandest mountain scenery in the world, let them drop in and look at the city of Lima, with its towering ranges of mountains on one side, and the gleaming ocean, with its rough and broken shore, on the other. Or if they have a desire to behold the gigantic and antique ruins of the ancient bow-and-gated city, they will find those presented with singular power and life in the Panorama of Thebes.—Evening Signal.

THE PANORAMA OF THEBES.

In this picture the observer is placed in the midst of the gigantic ruins of ancient Thebes—a city which, when in its splendor, was the capital of Egypt. Three thousand years ago it was in the height of its glory and prosperity, and is supposed to have contained two or three millions of people. Its ruins now cover a space of ten miles. The principal remains, which consist of the immense temples and palaces of Karnak, form the subject of the Panorama. Magnificent gateways, towering obelisks, and huge fragments of venerable edifices, are seen in every direction. To enliven the scene, and the melancholy feelings which fallen grandeur and general devastation lay upon the observer, the artist has introduced into the picture a caravan of pilgrims, with their camels and horses, which have just arrived from Cairo, preparing to encamp among the ruins. Several hundred figures are thus introduced, which have a most pleasing effect.

Thebes of the Hundred Gates.—We sat in our chariot, one and all, to treat themselves forthwith to a feast truly of this magnificent Panorama. It surpasses the wonderful ruins of the stupendous temples of Karnak—stupendous even in dilapidation—and giving testimony indeed, even when seen, the ideal not nearly comely, to the sensational colossal, wealth and praise of that mysterious people whose simple and history we are lost in the details of remote consumption upon. In this prior picture, everything and mighty as see the architectural marvel of Egyptian, worthies helots as a specimen only of the Egyptian edifices sponsored by Egyptian artists and labor; but what impression it is! What a system of Pagan—what exquisite supply of experiments—at mechanical ingenuity—the mediocrity of minds are left to us, when the scene is amply paintable this inspiration.—N. Y. Gazette.

Thebes, the ruined, but impenetrable city, whether you, the air of Sea of Shadow of Pharaoh and of Moses—the type of man's power, and time, and duration, in the earliest, forgotten that seen upon the wont and wonder.—Zion's Watchman.

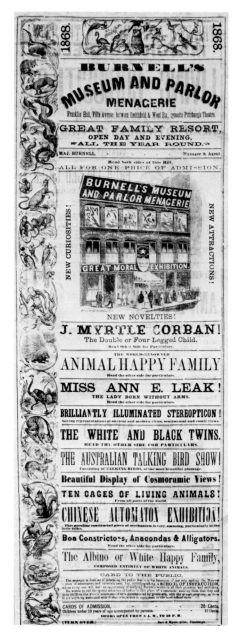

THE AMERICAN MUSEUM
BROADWAY, N. Y.
1850.

Circus has been with us in America since early Colonial times — in the simpler forms of menageries and acrobatic acts. People have always needed low-cost excitement and spectacle (witness today's television programming and the cult of the "disaster movie"). In the 19th century they found it in such establishments as the New York City Rotunda, Burnell's Museum and Parlour Menagerie, and, most especially, Barnum's American Museum. The last was perhaps the greatest attraction in America until its destruction by fire in 1868.

Barnum's American Museum; color engraving, 1850; Theatre Collection, The New York Public Library (photo: Thom Loughman)

OPPOSITE, LEFT: *Panorama of Lima and Thebes; broadside for the New York City Rotunda, 1846.* RIGHT: *"Burnell's Museum and Parlour Menagerie" (Pittsburgh); broadside, 1868; Somers (N.Y.) Historical Society (photo: Thom Loughman)*

General Tom Thumb; engraving by Nathaniel Currier, 1849; Somers (N.Y.) Historical Society (photo: Thom Loughman)

Court dress worn by Tom Thumb at a command performance for Queen Victoria, 1863; Somers (N.Y.) Historical Society (photo: Thom Loughman)

Phineas Taylor Barnum was truly a master showman. His museum featured a Moral Lecture Room where moral plays and farces were presented, sometimes as many as twelve in one day. Within the same building were such attractions as Tom Thumb, Japanese mermaids, equestrian shows, and many more innovative and unique presentations. Perhaps Barnum's most lucrative undertaking was the American tour of Jenny Lind, the Swedish Nightingale, whose advance publicity was so great that she sold out every concert in 137 cities and netted both herself and Barnum a fortune.

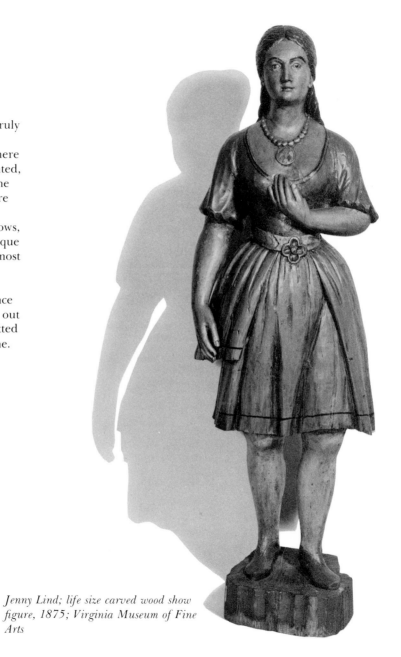

Jenny Lind; life size carved wood show figure, 1875; Virginia Museum of Fine Arts

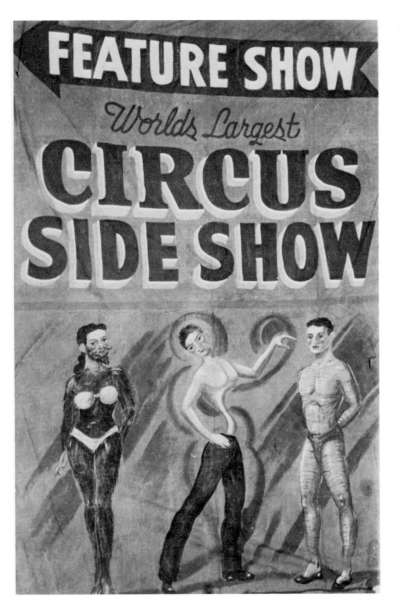

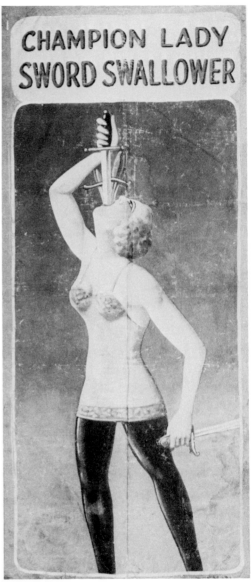

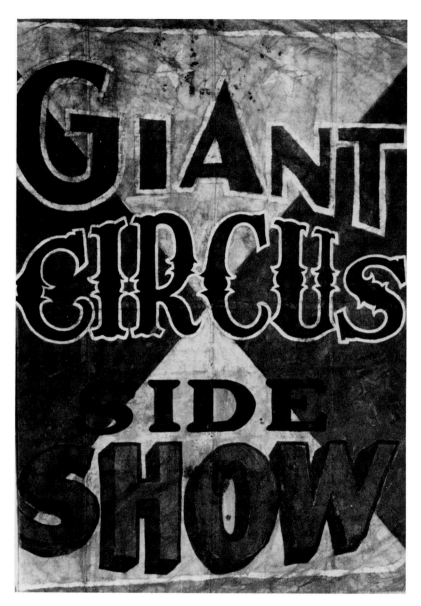

Carnival sideshow banners; painted canvas, early 20th century; collection of Sally R. Sommer (photo: Thom Loughman)

Barnum's influence in presenting the weird and exotic, though diminished, may never die. These sideshow banners were obtained in South Dakota in 1972 at the winter quarters of a working carnival. Though exotic attractions are greatly decreased in numbers from years past, some do remain, and there exists an appreciative audience. Whether one considers the carnival sideshow theatre or merely perversion, it must not be overlooked as an early form of entertainment which continues in our "sophisticated" society.

The Black Crook; *color lithograph poster, c.1860–70; Library of Congress*

Mazeppa; *color lithograph poster, c.1860–70; George J. Goodstadt, Inc. (photo: Thom Loughman)*

Mazeppa was perhaps the first play to offer the illusion of a nude woman on stage — this one strapped to the back of a live horse. The city was Albany; the woman, Adah Isaccs Menken; the year, 1861. (There is no information on the horse.) Both the play and the star were tremendously successful — and extremely scandalous. The culmination of feminine pulchritude on the 19th-century stage occurred in *The Black Crook.* In 1866, a French ballet company was unable to open at the New York Academy of Music because the theatre burned. William Wheatley, manager of Castle Garden, who was about to produce George Barras's *The Black Crook,* had the idea of incorporating the idle ballet troupe into his production — and although little was left of Barras's original script the numerous women in "close-fitting, flesh-colored tights" more than made up for the butchered text. *The Black Crook* ran for sixteen months and earned more than $1,100,000, although at least one critic marveled at its "scenic glories" and "unutterable stupidity." This poster represents one of numerous subsequent productions.

52

Painted canvas scenic drop from the Harmount Company production of Uncle Tom's Cabin, *1903–29; Theatre Research Institute, Ohio State University*

Uncle Tom's Cabin is perhaps the most successful of all American plays. Originally performed in 1852, it proved itself able to transcend the immediacy of the slavery debate and remained on the American stage until well into the 20th-century. Each new production offered increasingly spectacular scenic effects, more bloodhounds, and a younger and prettier Eva. The scenic drop pictured is from the production of the Harmount Company, which toured Ohio and the Midwest from 1903 until about 1930 as one of the last of Uncle Tom troupes.

Celery dish with a scene from H.M.S.
"Pinafore"; *produced by La Belle Glass
Works, Bridgeport, Ohio, c.1870; The
Boothbay Theatre Museum, Franklyn
Lenthall, Curator (photo: Thom
Loughman)*

The musical comedy has generally been recognized as a distinctly American art form. Many historians have found roots in European light operetta, represented by this piece of *H.M.S. "Pinafore"* "actress glass." I prefer, however, to think of Edward Harrigan as the originator. With female impersonator Tony Hart, Harrigan presented an entertaining yet accurate view of New York life among Irish and German immigrants. The popularity of Harrigan and Hart was immense, particularly among the people parodied in his productions. Harrigan's plays and their scores now make a strong case for native roots for our musical theatre. This rendering for *Squatter's Sovereignty* is by a scenic artist who worked for both Edward Harrigan and Edwin Booth.

Scenic rendering for Edward Harrigan's production of Squatter's Sovereignty *by Charles Witham, 1882; Theatre and Music Collection of the Museum of the City of New York (photo: Thom Loughman)*

Tired of singing in sleazy cafes and music halls, Tony Pastor opened a theatre in New York in 1865 with the intention of presenting the finest variety acts in an environment suitable for women and children. Its success can be said to be responsible for the later development of such revues as Ziegfeld's *Follies* — elaborate and decorative extensions of simple vaudeville presentations. These entertainments, which differed from the musical comedy in their lack of a story line, represent a distinctive theatrical form of immense popularity.

Tony Pastor; lithograph poster, c.1880; George J. Goodstadt, Inc. (photo: Thom Loughman)

GEO. L. FOX.

During the Civil War, George L. Fox's burlesques of Humpty Dumpty, Hamlet, and Macbeth were celebrated diversions for Union soldiers, and it is said that Fox performed Humpty Dumpty 1,268 times in New York alone. Burlesque took on a seamier side in later years. Though incorporating many of the elements of vaudeville (singing acts, comedy acts, jugglers, and acrobats), the primary focus of its "male only" audience was that "extra-added attraction" — the "hootchy kootchy" dancer. In later years, strip artists replaced these dancers to compete more aggressively with the motion picture for audiences. Although outlawed in New York in 1942, the peep shows and topless bars of today's Times Square proclaim burlesque as far from dead.

George L. Fox; lithograph poster, c.1880; George J. Goodstadt, Inc. (photo: Thom Loughman)

The Golden Age of the Manager

As we left the 19th and entered the 20th century, our nation and the world were rapidly changing. Trolley cars, automobiles and airplanes were mobilizing our people and expanding their world. Newspapers, magazines, and universities were broadening our cultural horizons. An excited and excitable public could create theatrical celebrities overnight — given the proper press, sufficient financial backing, and, of course, a modicum of talent.

Daniel Frohman began in the theatre as Steele MacKaye's business manager at the Madison Square Theatre. Two other brothers, Gustave and Charles Frohman, soon joined MacKaye's organization. Daniel assumed management of the MacKaye-built Lyceum Theatre in 1896, and soon after formed a stock company which served to introduce E. H. Sothern, Minnie Maddern Fiske, and, ironically, David Belasco, who was later to become the arch-rival of the Frohmans. However, it was Charles Frohman who truly epitomized the theatre of his time — and developed business practices still followed in our contemporary theatre. Beginning with his vastly successful production of Bronson Howard's *Shenandoah* in 1889, the American theatre was totally dominated by his presence until his death on the *Lusitania* in 1915. He controlled theatres, bought and sold plays on both sides of the Atlantic, and made stars overnight. *The Pageant of America* suggests the power of this exciting individual living in an exciting theatrical era: "In New York and London alone Frohman's theatres were worth over five million dollars. He paid thirty-five millions in salaries each year to upward of ten thousand employees; his yearly bill for advertising was over half a million; over three-quarters of a million was necessary to transport his troupes in their annual tours of America and Europe — with an extra half a million for baggage. . . ." And the list goes on.

Theatrical playing cards, c.1905; Theatre Collection, The New York Public Library, Astor, Lenox and Tilden Foundations (photo: Thom Loughman)

The Madison Square Theatre; from a souvenir booklet for Steele MacKaye's production of Hazel Kirke, *c.1880; Theatre Collection, The Free Library of Philadelphia (photo: Thom Loughman)*

To label an artist a visionary encourages thoughts of sainthood and martyrdom. Perhaps the label is accurate for Steele MacKaye. A designer, director, theatre manager, producer, actor, playwright . . . the list could go on to include every artistic capacity a man of the theatre can fill. He introduced Delsarte's unique method of acting to America. He gave David Belasco and the Frohmans their early training in the theatre. He built the Madison Square Theatre, the most beautiful and technically innovative theatre of its day; and he built the Lyceum Theatre, which still serves as a practical house with its splendor intact.

60

The MacKaye Spectatorium; watercolor by Childe Hassam, 1893; J. N. Bartfield Galleries and Schweitzer Gallery

Perhaps Steele MacKaye should be best known for a failure — the Spectatorium to be constructed at the Chicago World's Fair to house a pantomimic pageant chronicling the life of Columbus. It was to seat ten thousand spectators before twenty-five telescoping stages moved on miniature railroads. Its program called for the collaboration of the world's greatest theatrical, technical, musical, and artistic talents. MacKaye raised the capital and started construction. The Spectatorium was near completion when the financial panic of 1893 brought the project to a grinding halt — and the incomplete edifice was ultimately sold as scrap for $2,250. Steele MacKaye died the following year.

*Daniel Frohman; drawing by E. V.
Podherny, c.1910–1920; Actor's Fund of
America (photo: Thom Loughman)*

*At the Empire (Theatre); drawing by
Lesley Crawford, 1939; The Boothbay
Theatre Museum, Franklyn Lenthall,
Curator (photo: Thom Loughman)*

Daniel Frohman could not rival either Wallack or Daly in the overall quality of his Lyceum Theatre stock company productions. He did have a knack for presenting well acted and well staged plays which found broader popular acceptance than the classically oriented fare of his competitors. And financially, he was very shrewd — and very successful. His brother Charles opened his first New York theatre, the Empire, in 1893, after his huge success with *Shenandoah* (for which he had wisely arranged to purchase rights for even greater financial rewards on the road). The Empire was gorgeous. Its stock company's annual tour was an eagerly awaited nationwide event.

Peter Pan; *colored lithograph poster,*
1907; New-York Historical Society

Charles Frohman could not have developed stars without plays in which they could shine. He strove constantly to find and encourage new playwrights writing on popular subjects. William Gillette and Sir James Barrie were two of the writers whose work he produced regularly. Gillette, a popular actor as well as a writer, wrote melodramas — generally casting himself as a strong male lead. Among his best works were *Sherlock Holmes* and *Secret Service,* a spy melodrama set in the Civil War. Barrie, imported by Frohman from England, became such a good friend that the playwright served as Frohman's biographer after the producer's death. His two best-known works are *Peter Pan* and *The Admirable Crichton.*

Secret Service; *colored lithograph poster,*
1895; Library of Congress

63

Maude Adams; gilded china figurine, c.1890; The Boothbay Theatre Museum, Franklyn Lenthall, Curator (photo: Thom Loughman)

Maude Adams, a Frohman star whose career was made in the leading roles of Barrie's plays, was one of the most beloved personalities of her day. The degree of her exaltation is suggested in the prologue to *The Young Maude Adams* by Phyllis Robbins: "Just as the nineteenth century was turning into the twentieth, American newspapers carried a story like nothing that had ever been printed by them before. A life-sized statue made of solid gold from the famous Colorado mines at Cripple Creek was to tour the United States, and then be shipped to France as Colorado's exhibit at the Paris Exposition. It represented 'The American Girl.' One other golden girl comes to mind from Hawthorne's version for young Americans of the ancient myth of miserly King Midas . . . and his Golden Touch. Hawthorne — fine spinner of stories that he was — played around with the legend, and added a dramatic finish. . . . Midas's young daughter, who, . . . stiffened into gleaming metal at the fatal touch of her father's good-morning kiss. The statue of "The American Girl" was no legend; it was a very substantial fact, weighing seven hundred and twelve pounds, and valued at one hundred and twenty-five thousand dollars. Nor was it fashioned with a single touch, but painstakingly modeled by the sculptress Bessie Potter Vonnoh. The girl's pose was simple, standing with hands at her sides. She wore a plain evening dress with lace at the neck. Her hair was loosely gathered above her forehead. She was Maude Adams."

Ethel Barrymore (1879–1959) should need no introduction to any lover of the American theatre. A member of our most distinguished acting family, she achieved stardom on her own before coming under Frohman management. She was a versatile actress who had a long and distinguished career on the stage. She was also one of only two actresses (Helen Hayes being the other) to have a Broadway theatre named in her honor.

Richard Mansfield gained his early fame under Steele MacKaye at the Madison Square Theatre before performing in the second Frohman production at the Lyceum. From that time on, he was a favorite with Frohman's audiences in such roles as Dr. Jekyll and Cyrano, and as Beau Brummel in the play by Clyde Fitch, another popular Frohman playwright. Though sometimes faulted as a brittle and inflexible actor with little vocal variety, he took his art seriously and stood as an ethical model for the profession. This drawing is signed by Fred A. Kerley — Mansfield's butler.

The year following her marriage to Harrison Grey Fiske, New York journalist and dramatist, Minnie Maddern retired from the stage which had been a part of her life since age three. Fortunately, the retirement did not last. In subsequent years Mrs. Fiske became the major proponent of the works of Henrik Ibsen and a vocal force for greater realism. She represents an independent turn-of-the-century theatre in a battle waged against the theatrical "Syndicate."

The Syndicate was composed of Sam Nixon and Fred Zimmerman of Philadelphia, and Al Hayman, Charles Frohman, Marc Klaw and Abraham Erlanger of New York. These men owned most of the theatres in the country, controlled what was presented in them, and blocked performances by artists who did not bend to their conditions. From 1895–96 until 1905, when the Shuberts broke the Syndicate by forming an equally powerful opposition, actors who opposed their dictates were forced to perform in halls and tents. Mrs. Fiske opened her own small theatre to present such plays as *Leah Kleshna*.

For ten years David Belasco fought the Syndicate — his creativity as a playwright and director and the advances he made in the development of realistic scenic and lighting effects keeping him in public demand. In 1907 he opened his own theatre, the Belasco, with every possible technological innovation. The set model pictured is a good example of the attention to detail that characterized his productions. His success ultimately forced the Syndicate to accept him on his own terms.

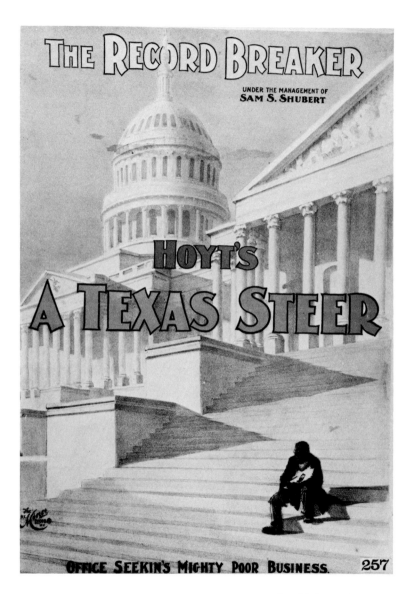

THE RECORD BREAKER

UNDER THE MANAGEMENT OF
SAM S. SHUBERT

HOYT'S
A TEXAS STEER

OFFICE SEEKIN'S MIGHTY POOR BUSINESS.   257

A Texas Steer; *colored lithograph poster;*
George J. Goodstadt, Inc. (photo: Thom
Loughman)

A Texas Steer was a broad farce by the popular playwright Charles Hoyt. It has little historical importance today other than as a stepping-stone toward the success of young Sam Shubert; and it serves here as introduction to what remains the Shubert brothers' theatrical empire.

In a true rags-to-riches development, the Shuberts (Sam, Lee, and J. J.) moved their small Syracuse operation to New York City and leased the Herald Square Theatre in 1900 — to begin their fight against the Syndicate. Through a combination of shrewd business dealings, sensible (if not adventurous) artistic judgment, and extreme competitiveness, they eventually destroyed the Syndicate — to become a monopolistic entity of infinitely greater size and strength. At the height of their power, the Shuberts owned and controlled about 90% of Broadway and about 75% of the theatres throughout the country.

Though the Shubert brothers have now passed away, their organization continues to operate numerous theatres around the country and in New York. The organization's involvement in production has diminished, but the philanthropic work of the Shubert Foundation continues as an important theatrical force.

Forty Five Minutes From Broadway; *sheet music cover, 1906; George M. Cohan Music Publishing Co. (photo: Thom Loughman)*

George Michael Cohan abandoned a profitable vaudeville career under the management of B. F. Keith — who, with Edward Albee (father of the playwright), had a hold over vaudeville much like the Frohman-Erlanger grip on legitimate theatre. Cohan made his Broadway debut at the age of 23, and continued on through a stormy and tempestuous career to become one of the most beloved actors and composers America has ever known. As a producer and manager he was fought by other producers and managers. As an actor, he opposed the formation of Actor's Equity and refused to participate in the strike of 1919 — because he was also a manager. But through it all, he won. Equity allowed him to perform without joining — a unique honor. His popularity as an actor, composer, and playwright kept the public coming to his theatre. As for his music — any music that can carry a nation through two World Wars and a Depression, which can last through more than half a century of vastly changing musical styles must be magical, written by a magical man. George M. Cohan's statue is in Duffy Square. His music is in our hearts.

The Yankee Doodle Boy; *sheet music cover, 1904; George M. Cohan Music Publishing Co. (photo: Thom Loughman)*

69

*James O'Neill as the Count of Monte Cristo;
color lithograph poster, c.1880–90; George
J. Goodstadt, Inc. (photo: Thom Loughman)*

*A Bernhardt billboard; photograph by
Edward J. Sullivan (Sarah Bernhardt's
American manager), c.1905–10; The
Boothbay Theatre Museum, Franklyn
Lenthall, Curator (photo: Thom
Loughman)*

Singing the praises of those that persevere successfully in the face of adversity is a joyous task. So it was with James O'Neill and Sarah Bernhardt. O'Neill was best known for his portrayal of the Count of Monte Cristo, which he performed thousands of times to the delight of his public — and his own distaste. Like most actors, he wanted to expand his art, but the Syndicate made it difficult for him to find bookings in other roles excepting in inadequate, nontheatrical spaces. His name was immortalized not by his own work, but by that of his son — Eugene Gladstone O'Neill.

Sarah Bernhardt, the great French tragic actress, made a habit of American farewell tours — nine of them in all. Her tour of 1905, sponsored by the Shubert brothers, ran into such intense Syndicate opposition that she was often forced to perform in tents.

Sarah Bernhardt as the Queen in Ruy Blas; *bronze statue, copyright 1879 by S. Kitson; The Boothbay Theatre Museum, Franklyn Lenthall, Curator (photo: Thom Loughman)*

Theatrical Craft into Dramatic Art

During the second decade of the 20th century, America's role in the world was drastically altered. Much of Europe's physical and cultural heritage was in shambles following the holocaust of World War I, and America was being looked to by the rest of the world as a source of stable leadership and support. Having undergone tremendous economic, industrial, and sociological changes during the late 19th and early 20th centuries, America was in a position to assume this mantle of responsibility — absorbing vast numbers of immigrants, doling out foreign aid, and developing unprecedented international trade.

Psychologically, these developments created a great strain on the moral fabric of the country. America was far from being a homogeneous nation, and the growing assimilation into the melting pot called for a period of self-examination. Communities, ethnic cultures, and religious and political groups each sought self-identification and preservation.

As Americans turned to their theatre to express their views and establish their identities, the theatre, as developed by the magnates of earlier years, proved incompatible with their needs; the Broadway "show" simply cost too much to mount, too much to travel, and (with the unionization of theatre) too much to run. Thus, communities turned within themselves to form smaller neighborhood theatres where productions done on a smaller scale and at a lower cost permitted a greater intimacy between performance and audience. During the season of 1928–29, commercial theatre persisted primarily in the spectacular musical revues of the Shuberts and Ziegfeld, but our best and most creative efforts came from the "little theatres." Modern playwriting, acting, and design all finally had a place to experiment freely, without fear of financial disaster. Eventually, the new artists infused a life into the Broadway scene which spoke to the nation — and the world.

The Almighty Dollar; *ink drawing by Hammond; Theatre Collection, The Free Library of Philadelphia (photo: Thom Loughman)*

World War I introduced America to concepts of theatre radically different from what was being presented on our home stages. British scenic artist Edward Gordon Craig and German designer Adolpha Appia were producing visually abstract works which allowed the actor and the play to dominate the stage. Lighting was better controlled, allowing for instantaneous scene changes while the curtain was raised. Dadaism, surrealism, and expressionism were part of the theatrical scene.

Symbolic of the new tradition, and perhaps the single most influential American scenic artist of all time, was Robert Edmond Jones. Jones was a writer, lecturer, director, and designer who, beginning with his work on Ashley Duke's *The Man Who Married a Dumb Wife* in 1915, created a revolution in American scenic art and production. The 19th-century romanticist's stage was conceived as a beautiful picture complete unto itself. The dedication of Jones's book *Drawings for the Theatre* — "To the Actor" — aptly expresses his opposition to the traditional concept. Jones's early work with the Provincetown Players, especially his designs for the plays of Eugene O'Neill, was particularly memorable. But his work found expression from the little theatres of Colorado to giant Broadway stages. Today, there is not a single production mounted which does not owe some gratitude to this great artist.

Top: *Scenic rendering for Ophelia's burial in* Hamlet *by Robert Edmond Jones — 1922 production starring John Barrymore; collection of Pat and Bud Gibbs (photo: Thom Loughman)*

Bottom: Below Stage: "The Green Pastures"; *watercolor by Don Freeman, 1930; Don Freeman is represented exclusively by The Margo Feiden Galleries, New York (photo: Thom Loughman)*

Left: *Scenic rendering for* The Green Pastures *by Robert Edmond Jones, 1930; collection of pat and Bud Gibbs (photo: Thom Loughman)*

Eugene Gladstone O'Neill is perhaps the most difficult American artist to assess and the most important with whom to come to grips. For through his work we can see an American soul being bared in self-exploration, going through a painful purging in an attempt to make us all more compassionate, more self-understanding people.

O'Neill's work on the stage began, after an abortive enrollment in Princeton, with George Pierce Baker's Harvard playwriting course in 1914–1915. In 1916, he was produced by the Provincetown Players, and in 1920 his first Broadway production, *Beyond the Horizon,* won the Pulitzer Prize and established him as a playwright of exceptional talent and promise. In the course of his career he won four Pulitzer Prizes and the Nobel Prize for literature.

These awards meant little to O'Neill. Neither did the financial rewards which came with success. In his work one sees a man searching for truth that comes only through the creative process. In his early plays he tended toward the melodramatic, slice-of-life situations. Soon he began experimenting with forms far more adventurous than any of his contemporaries: expressionism in *The Hairy Ape,* the use of masks in *The Great God Brown,* pageantry in *Marco Millions* and *Lazarus Laughed,* Freudian asides in *Strange Interlude.* His attempts were monumental in scope as well as form. One stands in awe at any production of *Mourning Becomes Electra,* six hours of intense psychological drama dealing with a New England family during the Civil War — based on Aeschylus's *Oresteia.*

Though the variety of forms and the sheer number of his works stand as a great tribute to O'Neill, it is what he said through his writings that is of the greatest importance. O'Neill wrote during a time of national introspection, and he wrote about things which were close to himself and, by nature, close to America — the sea, the farm, the place of man in a technological society, racial attitudes, and the perennial struggle of man and woman. Written by an American with an American outlook, his plays have proven to be as universal as those any playwright has ever written. The reader of his masterwork *Long Day's Journey Into Night* finds in its dedication the words "written in tears and blood." Until O'Neill, America was not ready to accept a play "written in tears and blood." O'Neill was able to face his own ghosts and see through to the future. American theatre was able to do the same.

Eugene O'Neill; bronze bust by Edmond T. Quinn; Yale School of Drama Library photo: Bruce Siddons

The opening of the Provincetown Playhouse in New York City in 1916 followed the precedent set by Winthrop Ames's Little Theatre (1912) and Alice and Irene Lewisohn's Neighborhood Playhouse (1915). Though the motivation for establishing them differed, they shared some basic artistic principles: an abhorrence for the commercial theatre, a high regard for the integrity of the playwright, and a belief in the theatre as an experimental forum with close links between the performers and the audience. These theatres and the later Washington Square Players took chances on plays and playwrights, giving voice to a new generation on the American stage.

Max Reinhardt's work was introduced to America in 1912 by a production of *Sumurun,* a wordless dance-music play incorporating much of the new stagecraft and lighting Reinhardt had been experimenting with in Europe. Reinhardt was experimental throughout his career, utilizing thrust and environmental staging, incorporating singers and dancers within an ensemble, and arranging massive crowd scenes with a realism never since equaled. His 1923 production of *The Miracle,* designed by Normal Bel Geddes, transformed New York's Century Theatre into a full-scale medieval cathedral and shattered the illusion of audience-actor separation. Following Hitler's takeover of his Berlin theatre, he came to America and became one of our leading stage and screen directors, creating the movie masterpiece *A Midsummer Night's Dream* for Warner Brothers in 1935.

S.S. "Glencairn" *window card for the Provincetown Playhouse, 1917; Beinecke Library, Yale University (photo: Thom Loughman)*

The Miracle; *lithograph by Carl Link, reproduced in* The New York Herald-New York Tribune *at Easter 1924; collection of Henry Marx (photo: Thom Loughman)*

For each new wave of immigrants that reached America, an ethnic theatre helped make the new land less harsh and more understandable. Of all these ethnic efforts, none had a more lasting effect on the development of the American art theatre than the Yiddish theatre movement. Many of our greatest actors, designers, and directors had their early training on Yiddish stages: Boris Aronson, Mordecai Gorelik, Jacob Ben-Ami, Paul Muni, Maurice Schwartz.

Yiddish theatres began to establish themselves in New York during the period of 1880–1890. The artists who arrived from Eastern Europe found an appreciative and hungry audience which sought ties with the "old country" to make for an easier adjustment and assimilation into the American system. But the artists also brought with them theatrical forms and practices heretofore unknown to American audiences and artists. Along with the performers came the influence of Stanislavski, German expressionism, impressionism, and other advanced and radical ideas.

Yiddish drama still appears periodically in New York. But with the Americanization of Jewish culture and the assimilation of the young away from the language and traditions of traditional Judaism, it can never reach the height of the influence it once achieved.

The scenic rendering for *The Final Balance* by David Pinsky, produced at the Unser Theatre in January 1922, is the first (or one of the first) productions designed by Boris Aronson after his arrival in America. Light and shadow and glimmering signs convey Aronson's early impressions of New York City.

Scenic rendering for The Final Balance *by Boris Aronson; collection of the designer (photo: Thom Loughman)*

JOSEPH·URBAN·ARCHITECT·EXECUTED·BY·JOSEPH·URBAN·THOMAS·W·LAMB·ARCHITECTS

*The Ziegfeld Theatre; charcoal drawing by
Hugh Ferriss, 1927; The Brander
Matthews Collection, Columbia University
(photo: Thom Loughman)*

82

Florenz Ziegfeld began producing simple revues of music and comedy intended to glorify the American woman in 1907. His extension of the Paris music hall and contemporary vaudeville was brought to fruition during the prosperous 1920s. Though competitors and imitations were rampant — Shubert's yearly *Artists and Models,* Earl Carroll's *Vanities* and *Sketchbooks,* and George White's *Scandals* — it was Ziegfeld who became the master producer of this form of entertainment. Ziegfeld's *Follies* became more spectacular as years progressed, and in the mid-twenties production costs soared to over a quarter of a million dollars — a large part going for elaborate settings and costumes decorated with real fur and jewels. The Ziegfeld Girl was synonymous with glamour.

With the opening of the Ziegfeld Theatre in 1927, New York had a showplace in keeping with the lavish quality of these productions. Ziegfeld could not combat the effects of the Depression, however, and the elaborate entertainment was soon to fade, never again to appear in so luxurious a form.

Curtain design for Ziegfeld's Follies of 1924 *by John Wenger; Theatre and Music Collection of the Museum of the City of New York (photo: Thom Loughman)*

Scenic model for Ziegfeld's Follies of 1927 *(the grand staircase scene) by Joseph Urban; The Brander Matthews Collection, Columbia University (photo: Thom Loughman)*

Scenic rendering for "The Blues" in George White's Scandals by Erte, 1926; Metropolitan Museum of Art, Gift of Jane Martin Ginsburg, 1967

Vaudeville, burlesque, revues, and the musical comedy were all booming in the 1920s. In 1927 alone one could have seen on Broadway Ziegfeld's productions of *Rio Rita* and *Showboat,* Eddie Cantor in Ziegfeld's *Follies,* Ed Wynn in *Manhattan Mary,* George M. Cohan in *The Merry Malones,* and Fred and Adele Astaire were in *Funny Face.*

The musical comedy of today — now recognized as a distinctive art form — can be traced back to these earlier forms.

Ed Wynn in Manhattan Mary; *Apollo Theatre, New York, 1927; drawing signed Firestone; Theatre Collection, The Free Library of Philadelphia (photo: Thom Loughman)*

W.C.Fields

"Eccentric Juggler..

Obituary.

W.C. Fields.

Born   Jan. 29. 1879

Died
April 20.08

Portland.
^and   Me.

Self-caricature of W. C. Fields; from "A Register of the Vaudeville Acts Appearing at the New Keith Theatre" in Portland, Maine, 1908; The Boothbay Theatre Museum, Franklyn Lenthall, Curator (photo: Thom Loughman)

Firestone

Our Contemporary Past

Attempting to place in historical perspective what has transpired in one's own lifetime is a difficult task. The major historical events and social movements are easily recognizable: the Depression, the Second World War, the rise of our technological society and the ensuing frustrations, the immersion of our society in television and mass media. All have had a demonstrable effect on the individual American and the fabric of American culture.

Theatrical developments are equally intertwined with the current character of the American people. Looking back at our contemporary past there are obvious highlights — the impact of our musical theatre as a truly indigenous art form; the playwrights like Odets, Miller, Williams, and Albee who followed O'Neill; the tremendous advances in theatrical architecture, design, and technology. To include one and exclude another from a survey such as this is a grievous, though necessary, predicament. So the following is a selection based on available works which will indicate only some of the highlights of our contemporary past.

Broadway has declined as the center of theatrical activity; Off-Broadway has risen and then fallen within two decades — succumbing to the same economic forces which affected the decline of Broadway. Regional theatres are increasing, as are summer stock and dinner theatres, many of these theatres producing original works which eventually find their way to the Broadway houses. The Off-Off Broadway movement is thriving — in New York, across the nation, and throughout the world — providing challenging plays and new playwrights, performers, and concepts of performance which seep into the mainstream of American theatre. Colleges and universities have become both the training ground and showcase for much of our new talent. And television and the movies continue to grow in power, prestige, and income — forcing a redefinition of what Americans want in their theatre.

Four scenic renderings for The Fabulous Invalid *by Donald Oenslager, 1938; Lent by Mrs. Donald Oenslager in memory of Donald Oenslager (photo: Thom Loughman)*

America has undergone many financial disasters, but none has had the impact or resultant consequences of the great Depression. Along with every other occupation in America, theatre artists were put out of work by the thousands during this bleak period.

Fortunately, Franklin Roosevelt and his administration had the foresight to see the people's need for the arts. By forming the Work Projects Administration and employing performing, visual, and other artists, the government provided culture to the general public and gave thousands of jobs to otherwise unemployed artists. The Federal Theatre Project, in existence between August 1935 and June 1939, was the first instance of government subsidy for artistic activity. It produced 830 major stage plays and over 6,000 radio plays while employing, at one time, over 12,000 people. Its significant innovations included The Living Newspaper dramatizations dealing with current events, early Black theatre, and classical plays performed with modern interpretation and setting. Among the Project's especially memorable efforts are the Welles-Houseman *Dr. Faustus,* early works by Arthur Miller, and the production of Sinclair Lewis's *It Can't Happen Here* — performed simultaneously in twenty-one cities. But it was the Living Newspaper productions like *One-Third of a Nation* which were most successful and influential — and which eventually led to the demise of the Federal Theatre Project as government responded to its political outspokenness. The Archives of the Federal Theatre Project are now being documented and preserved by George Mason University. The materials will be of incomparable significance to the historian as well as the theatrical artists of the future.

Costume rendering (the Cardinal) and production photo for Orson Welles' Dr. Faustus, *1937; Center for the Federal Theatre Project, George Mason University (photo: Thom Loughman)*

TOP RIGHT: One Third of a Nation; *production poster, 1938; Center for the Federal Theatre Project, George Mason University (photo: Thom Loughman)*

TOP FAR RIGHT: One Third of a Nation; *production photograph, 1938; Center for the Federal Theatre Project, George Mason University (photo: Thom Loughman)*

BOTTOM RIGHT: *Ground plan and scenic rendering for tent and battle scene in* Julius Caesar, *1937; Center for the Federal Theatre Project, George Mason University (photo: Thom Loughman)*

BOTTOM FAR RIGHT: Julius Caesar; *production photo, 1937; Center for the Federal Theatre Project, George Mason University (photo: Thom Loughman)*

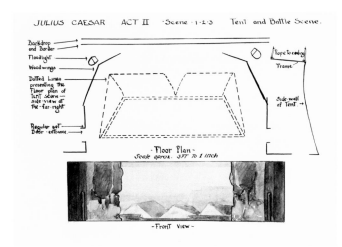

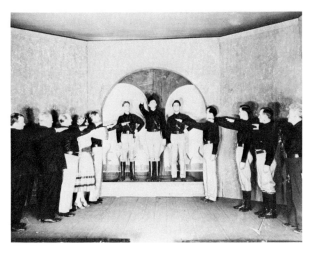

RIGHT: *Costume rendering for Paul Robeson's* Othello *by Robert Edmond Jones, 1943; Wesleyan University (photo: Thom Loughman)*

The Theatre Guild was established in 1919 as an offshoot of the Washington Square Players with the intention of presenting noncommercial plays on Broadway. Their audience was gathered on the basis of seasonal subscription. In later years, they developed audiences in many other cities on the same premise.

Though they had difficult times in the late 1930's and early 1940's, their impact on both the commercial and noncommercial American theatre was immense. Among the playwrights regularly presented by the Guild were George Bernard Shaw, A. A. Milne, Elmer Rice, Luigi Pirandello, Sidney Howard, Eugene O'Neill, Maxwell Anderson, and, of course, William Shakespeare. Actors who were associated with the Guild included Alfred Lunt and Lynne Fontanne, Ruth Gordon, Helen Hayes, Paul Robeson, Alla Nazimova, and Katherine Hepburn. Designers who worked for the Guild included Jo Mielziner, Lee Simonson, Robert Edmond Jones, Aline Bernstein, and Stewart Chaney. The Guild presented some of the most innovative and influential of all musicals, including *Porgy and Bess, Carousel,* and the landmark *Oklahoma.*

The Theatre Guild still does an occasional production, but its heyday went with the passing of its original board of directors. However, the standards it set and the policies it developed to intermingle noncommercialism in the commercial theatre are looked upon with envy by every contemporary producer.

The Theatre Guild also spawned The Group Theatre, which produced Maxwell Anderson's *Night Over Taos,* Sidney Kingsley's *Men in White,* and the work of a young playwright named Clifford Odets.

Alfred Lunt and Lynn Fontanne in The Taming of the Shrew; *O/C by Cristina Perry, c.1935; The Brander Matthews Collection, Columbia University (photo: Thom Loughman)*

RIGHT: Oklahoma; *production photo, 1943; The Library of Congress*

FAR RIGHT: *Scenic rendering for* Men in White *by Mordecai Gorelik; Southern Illinois University Special Collections*

90

The New York Times said "sooner or later everyone will have to see *Life With Father*" — and sooner or later almost everyone did. The play by Howard Lindsay and Russel Crouse (starring Lindsay and Dorothy Stickney) opened in 1939 and ran for seven years.

Life With Father; *lithograph by Don Freeman; Don Freeman is represented exclusively by The Margo Feidern Galleries, New York City (photo: Thom Loughman)*

Scenic rendering for A Streetcar Named Desire *by Jo Mielziner, 1947; on loan from Elia Kazan to the Theatre Collection, The New York Public Library, Astor, Lenox and Tilden Foundations (photo: Peter A. Juley & Son)*

Tennessee Williams had already risen to high stature in American playwriting with *The Glass Menagerie* before *A Streetcar Named Desire* opened on Broadway at the Barrymore Theatre. But the quality of performances by Marlon Brando, Karl Malden, Kim Hunter and Jessica Tandy as directed by Elia Kazan undoubtedly helped Williams toward the Pulitzer Prize for playwriting in 1948 and cemented his position for the future.

Scenic rendering for The Member of the Wedding *by Lester Polakov, 1950; collection of the designer (photo: Thom Loughman)*

The Member of the Wedding is more a character study from the Carson McCullers novel than a play with a typical dramatic form. However, the characters were so fully formed and developed by both the playwright and the cast of the original production that they captivated the hearts and minds of America and gave a tremendous boost to the careers of Ethel Waters and Julie Harris.

Ethel Waters in The Member of the Wedding; *O/C by Lester Polakov, 1950; The Brander Matthews Collection, Columbia University (photo: Thom Loughman)*

J. B., a retelling of the story of Job in dramatic form by Archibald MacLeish, twice a winner of the Pulitzer Price for poetry, was performed at the Yale School of Drama before being seen on Broadway in 1958. The Broadway production — with Raymond Massey and Christopher Plummer, directed by Elia Kazan and with Boris Aronson as designer — won a Tony award as the best dramatic play of 1958 and garnered Mr. MacLeish a third Pulitzer Prize in 1959 — this one for playwriting.

Scenic rendering for J.B. *by Boris Aronson, 1958; collection of the designer (photo: Robert Galbraith)*

J.B.; *photograph of the set designed by Boris Aronson, 1958; collection of the designer (photo: Robert Galbraith)*

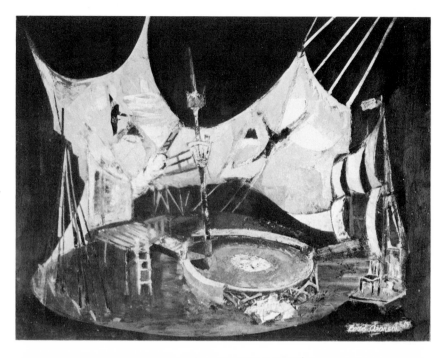

Of Thee I Sing (1931) was a satirical musical about the attempt to elect John P. Wintergreen president of the United States on a platform of love. A stinging satire which was widely hailed, it had a book by George S. Kaufman, and Morris Ryskind, music by George Gershwin, lyrics by Ira Gershwin, and settings by Jo Mielziner — all of whom are pictured in this rehearsal scene.

Of Thee I Sing; lithograph by Don Freeman, 1931; Don Freeman is represented exclusively by The Margo Feiden Galleries, New York City (photo: Thom Loughman)

The *Lady in the Dark* was Gertrude Lawrence, visiting her psychiatrist and recalling images from her past in an attempt to make sense of her life. It was one of the first of a new theatrical genre in which musical interludes are woven into the fabric of the script as an integral dramatic element. The play was written and directed by Moss Hart, with music by Kurt Weill, lyrics by Ira Gershwin, and scenery by Harry Horner. It was an effectively executed blend of the real and the expressionistic, and marked a great step forward for the American theatre of 1941.

Scenic rendering for the Park Avenue hotel in Lady in the Dark *by Harry Horner, 1940; collection of the designer*

Ethel Merman as Annie Oakley; oil and acrylic on canvas by Rosemarie Sloat, 1971; National Portrait Gallery, Smithsonian Institution

Laffing Room Only; *drawing by Al Hirschfeld, 1944; Al Hirschfeld is represented exclusively by The Margo Feiden Galleries, New York City (photo: Thom Loughman)*

Ole Olsen and Chic Johnson were two vaudevillians who had a tremendous success in 1938 with a "scream-lined revue" named *Hellzapoppin* — which was completely loony, ran for years, and earned tons of money for Olsen, Johnson, and Lee Shubert. The understated opening of Brooks Atkinson's review — "it is going to be a little difficult to describe this one" — tells all. *Laffing Room Only* can be considered the sequel to *Helzapoppin.*

Annie Get Your Gun (1946) had two good things going for it: Irving Berlin's music and Ethel Merman's performance. Scenery and lighting by Jo Mielziner, costumes by Lucinda Ballard, the direction of Joshua Logan, and all the supporting cast tend to go unnoticed when Ms. Merman takes the stage to sing a Berlin song.

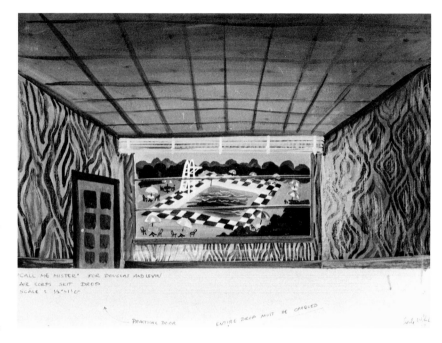

Irving Berlin wrote still another musical during World War II — this one with an all-soldier cast and entitled *This Is the Army.* Harold Rome, while himself in the service, conceived of a musical revue about what would happen to all the soldiers who returned home and had to adjust to civilian life. His *Call Me Mister,* with book by Arnold Auerbach and Arnold Herwitt, performed and produced by an all-veteran cast and crew, opened in 1946 and was lauded for its strength in dealing with the social and political issues inherent in its theme. It ran for 734 performances.

97

Little need be said about Allan Jay Lerner and Frederick Loewe's masterpiece, *My Fair Lady.* From its opening on March 15, 1956, until the end of its 2,717 performances, an historic episode of the American musical theatre was on view. A skillful adaptation of one of our greatest contemporary plays, George Bernard Shaw's *Pygmalion,* it stands as perhaps the most popular musical ever written.

Scenic rendering for My Fair Lady *by Oliver Smith, 1956; collection of the designer (photo: Thom Loughman)*

Scenic rendering for the "rumble" in West Side Story *by Oliver Smith, 1957; collection of the designer (photo: Thom Loughman)*

West Side Story was the conception of choreographer-director Jerome Robbins and composer Leonard Bernstein. Their attempt to turn the classic tale of Romeo and Juliet into a modern, true-to-life story of the love of a white youth for an Hispanic girl set against the background of urban street gang warfare was successful in every aspect: the tragedy was transferred intact, the music was an essential element of the story, and the mixture of ballet and modern dance was artfully handled to be in keeping with the nature of the characters. It was a musical of historical immediacy which took our theatre one step closer to perfection.

A musical with a long title, *A Funny Thing Happened on the Way to the Forum* — with book by Burt Shevelove and Larry Gelbart, lyrics and music by Stephen Sondheim — won the Tony award for best musical of 1962. Based on the plays of Plautus, it gave Zero Mostel and Jack Gilford, two of America's greatest comic actors, an ideal opportunity to display their talents.

Scenic model for A Funny Thing Happened On the Way to the Forum *by Tony Walton, 1962; collection of the designer (photo: Thom Loughman)*

Preliminary rendering for the wedding scene in Fiddler on the Roof *by Boris Aronson, 1964; Theatre and Music Collection of the Museum of the City of New York (photo: Thom Loughman)*

Fiddler on the Roof was another musical adaptation, this one based on the works of Sholom Aleichem and, again, starring Zero Mostel. Set in czarist Russia during the era of Jewish pogroms, the play had a touching immediacy similar in effect to *West Side Story,* and, like it, was staged by Jerome Robbins.

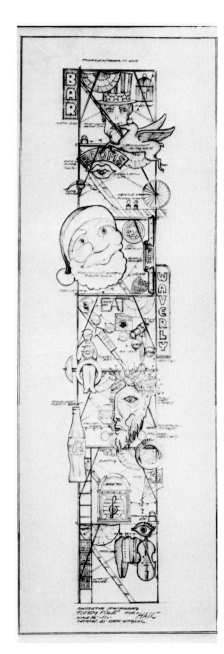

Rendering for the scaffolding totem pole in Hair *by Robin Wagner, 1967; collection of the designer (photo: Thom Loughman)*

It was inevitable that rock music would eventually infiltrate the Broadway stage. *Hair* was the advance scout — with book (what there was of one) and lyrics by Gerome Ragni and James Rado and music by Galt MacDermot. It was produced at the New York Shakespeare Festival's Public Theatre, with Gerald Freedman directing and Ming Cho Lee as the designer, before being transferred to Broadway on April 29, 1968, with Tom O'Horgan directing and Robin Wagner designing. "The American tribal love-rock musical" was loud, crude — and extremely effective.

Following the success of *Hair* came *Jesus Christ Superstar,* the first rock opera. This story of the life of Jesus of Nazareth was effective largely because of Tom O'Horgan's imaginative staging, Ben Vereen's performance as Judas, the visual effects of Jules Fisher's lighting and Randy Barcelo's costumes, and a truly beautiful score.

Death mask and death mask rendering for Jesus Christ Superstar *by Randy Barcelo; collection of the designer (photo: Thom Loughman)*

100

Follies was a semisweet tribute to the genre of its title. A poignant musical, reminiscing about the death of an art form and the lives of those who once were Follies girls, it took six Tony awards in 1972, including the fifth won by Boris Aronson during his distinguished career in the theatre. Other awards were given to Florence Klotz for her costumes, Harold Prince and Michael Bennett for direction and choreography, Stephen Sondheim for the score, and Alexis Smith for best actress in a musical.

Pacific Overtures was the first production to open on Broadway in 1976. Another Prince-Aronson-Sondheim-Klotz endeavor, it uses traditional Broadway forms intermixed with Kabuki theatre to tell the story of Perry's opening of Japan to the West.

Costume rendering for Follies *by Florence Klotz; collection of the designer (photo: Thom Loughman)*

Costume rendering for Pacific Overtures *by Florence Klotz, 1976; collection of the designer (photo: Thom Loughman)*

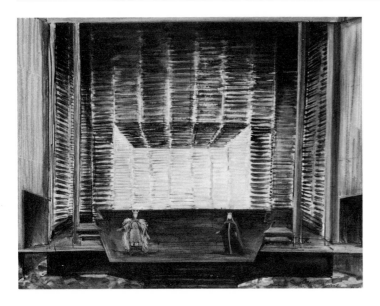

The Barter Theatre; drawing by Al Hirschfeld; Al Hirschfeld is represented exclusively by The Margo Feiden Galleries, New York City (photo: Thom Loughman)

Rendering for King John *(1956) on the 1952–59 festival stage at the American Shakespeare Festival, Stratford, Connecticut, by Rouben Ter-Arutunian, 1956; collection of the designer (photo: Thom Loughman)*

Two scenic renderings for Waiting for Godot *by Albert Johnson, 1955; collection of Alan Schneider (photo: Thom Loughman)*

Regional theatre traces back to the earliest colonial companies which established themselves in the budding metropolises of our nation. However, it is only in the wake of the 20th-century little theatre movement that small (and some not so small) regional playhouses have become artistic forces serving their communities with quality productions and serving theatre in general by training playwrights, actors, designers, and directors in professional situations without the pressures of Broadway. The theatres represented here are but two examples of the abundant regional theatres now in operation. The Barter Theatre of Abingdon, Virginia, established in 1933 when acting jobs were virtually nonexistent because of the Depression, enabled the hill farmers who constituted its primary audience to pay for tickets with an equal value of produce or livestock. It exists today as the State Theatre of Virginia and, over the years, has given us many fine performers who trained on its boards. The American Shakespeare Festival in Stratford, Connecticut opened in 1955 as a permanent home for the bard in America. As with most nonprofit theatres in operation today, it is in financial trouble.

One of the greatest of all contemporary plays was introduced to America in a regional theatre before making its New York appearance — *Waiting for Godot* by Samuel Beckett, staged by Alan Schneider, designed by Albert Johnson, and starring Bert Lahr, first seen at the Coconut Grove Playhouse in Miami, Florida, January 4, 1956.

Scenic model for Raisin *by Robert U. Taylor; collection of Robert Nemiroff (photo: Thom Loughman)*

Among the most prolific regional organizations in the development of plays which eventually come to Broadway is the Arena Stage in Washington, D.C. Founded and run by Ms. Zelda Fichandler, it has been in operation since 1950 and is the oldest resident theatre on the East coast. Pictured here are scenic models for two Broadway productions originally presented at the Arena — Arthur Kopit's *Indians*, and *Raisin*, the musical adaptation of Lorraine Hansbury's *Raisin in the Sun*.

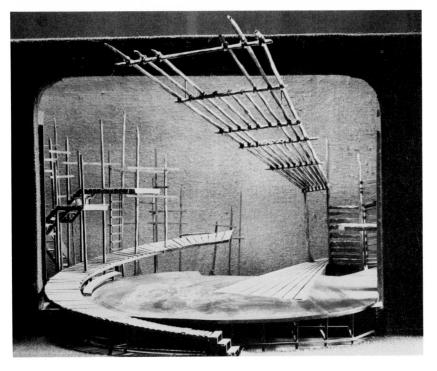

Scenic model for Indians *by Oliver Smith, 1969; collection of the designer (photo: Thom Loughman)*

Scenic rendering for The Rise and Fall of the City of Mahagonny *by Tony Straiges, 1975; courtesy of the designer and the Yale Repertory Theatre (photo: Thom Loughman)*

Schools and colleges have recently taken an important place as a training ground for theatrical artists. Nearly every major college in America has a growing theatre program, and most of the best new theatres built in America during the last two decades have been for universities. Though most colleges have traditionally encouraged and sponsored theatre, it is only recently that permanent professional companies have been established to allow students to work with professional actors while still studying for their degrees. The Yale Repertory Theatre is well known for developing numerous playwrights, actors, and designers who have gone on to high acclaim.

Scenic rendering for The Effects of Gamma Rays on Man in the Moon Marigolds *by Fred Voelpel, 1965; collection of the designer (photo: Thom Loughman)*

The Off-Broadway movement, like the regional theatre movement, is actually an extension of the little theatres of the early 20th century. The Neighborhood Playhouse and the Provincetown Playhouse were essentially Off-Broadway theatres in philosophy and practice. However, the contemporary Off-Broadway theatre stems from the Circle in the Square 1952 production of Tennessee William's *Summer and Smoke.* The original aim was to experiment away from the expensive commercialism of Broadway; but today's Off-Broadway theatre is so unionized and regulated that its production costs almost equal those of Broadway — and it is therefore rapidly fading.

At its peak, Off-Broadway theatre produced important plays, brought up challenging ideas, and showcased some of today's greatest talent. Paul Zindel's *The Effect of Gamma Rays on Man-In-The Moon Marigolds* (1965) was the only Off-Broadway show to ever win a Pulitzer Prize. *The Boys in the Band* was the first broadly successful play dealing with homosexuality.

Scenic model for The Boys in the Band *by Peter Harvey, 1968; collection of the designer (photo: Thom Loughman)*

Costume renderings for The Old Glory *by Willa Kim, 1964; collection of the designer (photo: Thom Loughman)*

The American Place Theatre began as an Off-Off Broadway effort in 1964. It has been vastly successful and is now housed in a new Times Square area theatre. Though almost literally "on" Broadway, it has become and remains an Off-Broadway house, with ticket sales by subscription only. It proclaims that "The American Place Theatre exists to foster good writing for the theatre." With plays like *The Old Glory*, it lives up to its promise.

The Old Glory; *production photograph by Martha Holmes, 1964; courtesy of the American Place Theatre (photo: Thom Loughman)*

Scenic rendering for the Delacorte Theatre production of Love's Labors Lost *by Ming Cho Lee, 1965; collection of the designer (photo: Thom Loughman)*

The New York Shakespeare Festival began as a small Off-Off Broadway effort in 1957, and has expanded under the guidance of Joseph Papp to involve all aspects and levels of theatrical activity. At the present time, Papp is the most important force in the American theatre.

Initially, the purpose of the Festival was to present free Shakespeare to the people of New York. That purpose is still fulfilled through summer performances at Delacorte Theatre in Central Park. Operations now also include citywide touring productions of the Mobile Theatre, productions on the numerous stages of the downtown Public Theatre, the operation of two Lincoln Center theatres — and productions on Broadway itself!

Among the most important plays presented by The New York Shakespeare Festival (many of which went on to commercial Broadway success) were *Hair, No Place to be Somebody, The Basic Training of Pavlo Hummel,* the musical *Two Gentlemen of Verona* (originally a free production in Central Park), *That Championship Season, Sticks and Bones,* and *A Chorus Line.* Actors who have adorned the Festival's many stages include Colleen Dewhurst, Julie Harris, Nan Martin, Frank Silvera, James Earl Jones, Stacy Keach, James Ray, and Kathleen Widdoes.

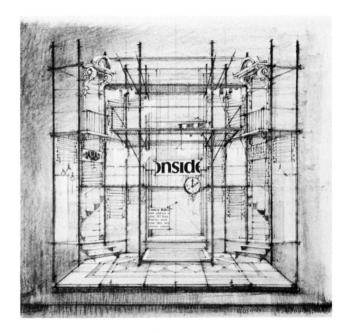

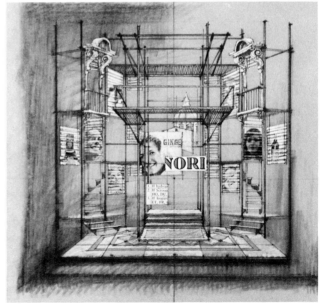

Scenic renderings for Two Gentlemen of Verona *by Ming Cho Lee; courtesy of the designer and The New York Shakespeare Festival (photo: Thom Loughman)*

Portents for the Future

Today's experimental theatre points the way to a lively future. The Off-Off Broadway movement started in the 1960's with such groups as the Living Theatre, the Open Theatre, Cafe Cino, and Cafe La Mama. Their original intention, like most little theatre movements before them, was to allow playwrights a chance to be produced and to develop in an environment free from commercialism. What has allowed Off-Off Broadway to expand and grow in importance over the years and avoid the assimilation that terminated preceding experiments was the acceptance by government and private foundations of the need for subsidies to prevent artistic compromise. For years this movement has been the most vital training ground and producing force in the American theatre.

The true significance of the experimental theatre lies with those participants who take our impending state of world crisis seriously and attempt to find forms which can supply what man needs and wants from his theatre in a changing society. Some do not accept the concept of the passively observant audience, and are seeking new forms and performance environments in which the audience is forced to respond and participate. Some play with time, seeking a redefinition of theatrical time more in keeping with our age of jet lag, destroying the viewer's normal time sense through elongated movement and speech until the performance time becomes confused with real time. Some are experimenting with language, attempting to find a means of communication understood by African aborigines as well as New York sophisticates. All of the experimental artists define the theatre as a laboratory, with the audience as much a part of the process as the actors.

Whether any of these forms or concepts will persist in the future remains to be seen. If commercial acceptance is the criterion, the introduction of environmental staging in *Candide* or the performance of Robert Wilson's *A Letter to Queen Victoria* on Broadway can be construed as the legitimatizing of the experimental. But laboratories and workshops without commercial involvement have thrived in pure form for many years. Our nation's theatre had its beginnings in the converted lofts,

Improvisation based on the Living Theatre's production of Paradise Now, *1969 (photo: Max Waldman — Gruenebaum Gallery, Ltd.)*

111

breweries, and warehouses of the colonial period. It is ironic that the future of our stage has retrenched in similar spaces. But whereas the Hallam Company gave its audience what was wanted as defined by centuries of tradition, our contemporary artists are giving the audience what the artists feel they need.

Rocky Greenberg, George Kon, and Scott Duncan in the Iowa Theater Lab production of Moby Dick *(photo: Ric Zank)*

The Iowa Theatre Lab, which was started in 1970 at the University of Iowa's Center for New Performing Arts, is now located in Baltimore, Maryland. It aims to develop an intimate form of theatre for a young, deeply committed audience through close physical and emotional contact between performer and spectator. Its work centers on the actor — with very little use of costume, property, or scenic effect. The Lab's repertory is developed through improvisation to allow a more personal tie between the actor and the material.

112

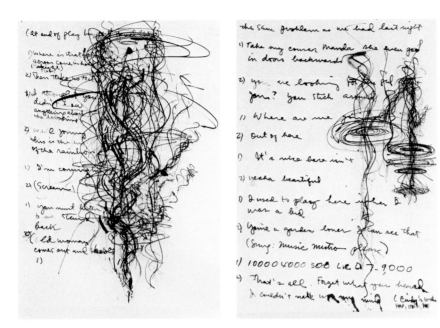

Robert Wilson is an artist who experiments with time and language at The Byrd Hoffman School of Byrds in SoHo. His work is visually stunning and totally perplexing, with scraps of dialogue and nonsensical series of words defying any accepted frame of theatrical reference. His actors are artists, dancers, businessmen, grandmothers, infants, the physically handicapped, and people off the street. His works have been performed by command for the Queen of Iran and at major European festivals as well as in his small studio-loft. His praise has been worldwide, though few traditional critics can explain what it is that Mr. Wilson is truly attempting.

A Letter to Queen Victoria: four pages from Robert Wilson's production notebook, 1975; courtesy of the Byrd Hoffman Foundation (photo: Thom Loughman)

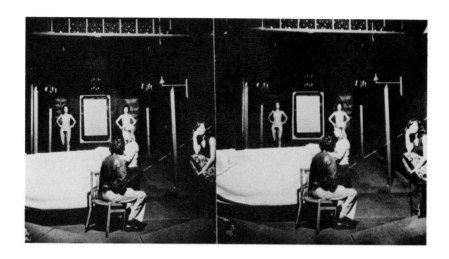

Richard Foreman directs and writes for his Ontological-Hysteric Theatre in SoHo. Another manipulator of time and language, his work is difficult for the uninitiated to assimilate, often monotonous, and lacking any traditional sense of drama. However, the tedium of his plays tends to make the viewer forget about normal speech, movement, and behavior; and, once accepted, they become puzzlingly moving and rich in their starkness.

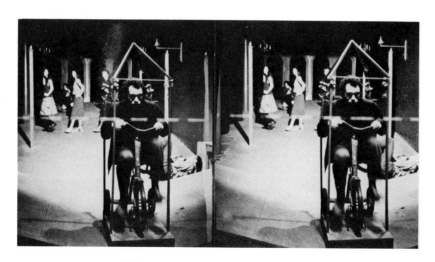

Costume for Carla the Gypsy Woman from The Ridiculous Theatrical Company's production of Turds in Hell, *1969; designed and modelled by Mario Montez; A Bunch of Experimental Theatres of New York, Inc. (photo: Thom Loughman)*

Charles Ludlum writes, directs, and stars in the productions of The Ridiculous Theatrical Company. In many ways his productions are a throwback to the 19th century — in reliance on a stock company (with Ludlum as star), the use of burlesque forms to parody classic plays, and the melodramatic costume, scenery, and lighting. His comic style is unique, drawing from vaudeville routines, oriental theatre, silent movies, and circus sideshows. One of the few experimentalists to rely on a proscenium stage, he is truly the clown prince of the underground.

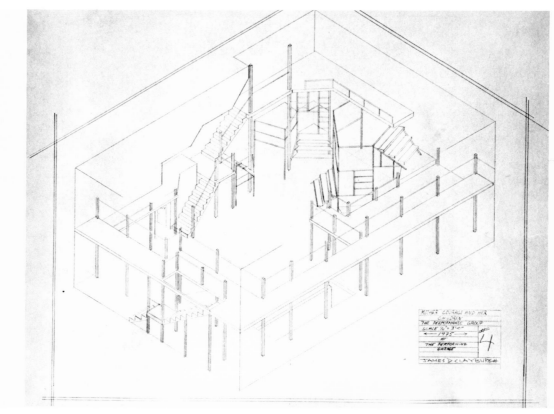

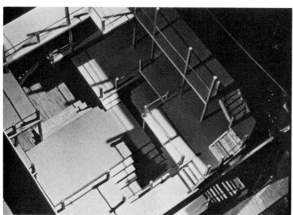

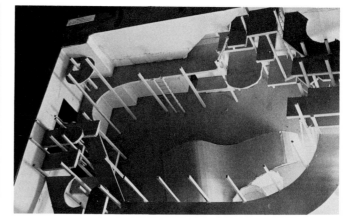

LEFT: *Environmental rendering for* Mother Courage and Her Children *by James D. Clayburgh, 1975; collection of the designer (photo: Thom Loughman)*

RIGHT: Mother Courage and Her Children, *1975 (photo: Pamela Shandel)*

BOTTOM, FAR LEFT: *Fixed environmental model for the Mobius Theatre, The University of Connecticut, by Jerry Rojo; collection of the designer*

BOTTOM LEFT: *Environmental model for* Commune *by Jerry Rojo; collection of the designer (photo: Barry Rimler)*

BOTTOM RIGHT: Commune *(photo: Pamela Shandel)*

The Performance Group, founded in 1967 by Richard Schechner, is today a collaborative ensemble experimenting with the relationships between performer, audience, space, text, and time. All roles of actor, director, designer, and crew are interchangeable within the group. Their innovations in environmental staging and flexible performance space have been assimilated into recent Broadway shows, and they have been responsible for the development of new modular theatres at colleges throughout the country. Among their most highly acclaimed works are *Commune, Dionysus in 69, The Tooth of Crime,* and *Mother Courage and Her Children.*

Scenic rendering for The Dybbuk *by David Hays; collection of Jean Leslie Worth (photo: Thom Loughman)*

The National Theatre of the Deaf was formed by David Hays (a leading Broadway designer) under the auspices of the Eugene O'Neill Memorial Theater Center in 1967. Using elements of speech, sign language, pantomime, and dance, the National Theatre for the Deaf has created an artistically successful mode of communication for the hearing as well as the deaf — a fully comprehensible form of theatre of lasting importance.

The Saint and the Football Players is a performance piece by Mabou Mines which examines the theatricality of sport through out-of-context use of football images, rituals, and traditions. Sports events, being the most popular form of contemporary performance, are a natural focus for such dissection. When captured on tape, the seemingly divergent elements of video, sports, and theatre are formed into an artistic unit — to further expand the definition and boundaries of American theatre.

Mabou Mines The Saint and the Football Players; *production conceived and directed by Lee Breuer; videotape by Jaime Caro; courtesy of A Bunch of Experimental Theatres (photo: Thom Loughman)*

Lenders

Actors Fund of America; Altman Stage Lighting Company; American Shakespeare Festival; Boris Aronson; Mr. and Mrs. Robert Ballard; Randy Barcelo; Barter Theatre; J. N. Bartfield Galleries, Inc.; Blaine-Thompson Advertising Company; Boothbay Theatre Museum; Brooks-Van Horn Costume Company; A Bunch of Experimental Theatres, Inc.; The Byrd-Hoffman Foundation; California Historical Society; James D. Clayburgh; George M. Cohan Music Publishing Co.; Pearl and Carl Cohen; Colonial Williamsburg; Columbia University, Department of Art Properties and The Brander Matthews Collection; Cooper-Hewitt Museum of Design, Smithsonian Institution; David Davies; Eaves Costume Company, Inc.; The Margo Feiden Galleries; The Free Library of Philadelphia, Theatre Collection; Pat and Bud Gibbs; George J. Goodstadt, Inc.; Mordecai Gorelik; Gruenebaum Gallery, Ltd.; Harvard University, Harvard Theatre Collection; Peter Harvey; Historical Society of York County; Harry Horner; Institute of the American Musical; Shirley Kaplan; Kent State University Special Collections; Willa Kim; Fred Kolouch; Ming Cho Lee; Library of Congress; Philip H. Likes, II; Santo Loquasto; Louisiana State Museum; Kert Lundell; Henry Marx; Metropolitan Museum of Art; Jo Mielziner; Museum of the City of New York, Theatre and Music Collection; National Archives; National Parks Service (Ford's Theatre National Historic Site); National Portrait Gallery, Smithsonian Institution; Neighborhood Playhouse School of the Theatre; Robert Nemiroff; New-York Historical Society; New York Public Library (Prints Division and Theatre Collection), Astor, Lenox and Tilden Foundations; New York Shakespeare Festival; Mrs. Donald Oenslager; Ohio State University, Theatre Research Institute; Ralph Pendleton; Pennsylvania Academy of Fine Arts; Lester Polakov; Portfolio Productions; Princeton University Theatre Collection; Carl H. Rohman; Jerry Rojo; Saint Subber Productions; Alan Schneider; Schweitzer Gallery; Sleepy Hollow Restorations, Inc.; Anthony Slide; Somers Historical Society; Sally R. Sommer; Southern Illinois University, Special Collections; Oliver Smith; Rouben Ter-Arutunian; Theatre Art Books; Trinity Square Repertory Theatre; University of Texas at Austin, Humanities Research Center; Virginia Museum of Fine Arts; Fred Voelpel; Robin Wagner; Max Waldman; Tony Walton; Wesleyan University; Jean Worth; Yale University, Beinecke Library, Yale Repertory Theatre, and Yale School of Drama.

Bibliography

Coad, Oral Sumner and Edwin Mims, Jr.
The Pageant of America: The American Stage.
New Haven: Yale University Press, 1929.

Henderson, Mary C.
The City and the Theatre.
Clifton: James T. White, 1973.

Hunter, Frederick J.
A Guide to the Theatre and Drama Collections at the University of Texas.
Austin: Humanities Research Center, 1967.

McNamara, Brooks.
The American Playhouse in the Eighteenth Century.
Cambridge: Harvard University Press, 1969.

Museum of the City of New York.
Stars of the New York Stage.
New York City: Friends of the Theatre and Music Collection, 1970.

National Portrait Gallery.
Portraits of the American Stage: 1771–1971.
Washington: Smithsonian Press, 1971.

Theatre Library Assoc. Ted Perry, ed.
Performing Arts Resources, Vol. 1.
NYC: Drama Book Specialists, 1974.

Wilson, Garff B.
Three Hundred Years of American Drama and Theatre: From "Ye Bear and Ye Cubb" to "Hair."
Englewood Cliffs: Prentice-Hall, 1973.

Young, William C.
Theatrical Arts: A Guide to Manuscripts and Special Collections in the United States and Canada.
Chicago: American Library Assoc., 1970.

Young, William C.
Documents of American Theatre History. 2 vols.
Chicago: American Library Assoc., 1973.

DESIGNED BY WINSTON POTTER